Ross was close enough to hear the hitch in Amanda's breath.

"You put yourself in danger tonight for a story," he said. "You will never do that again, or I will fire you. Understand?"

She nodded, and her lips trembled, and he felt something inside him soften toward her. He wanted to…kiss her.

Back off, he commanded himself. It would be a mistake. Even if he weren't pursuing a story that might lead directly to her father, he couldn't get involved with someone who worked for him.

Amanda, despite her veneer of sophistication, was really a small-town girl at heart. She was the sort of person who believed in love and fidelity and happily-ever-after. All the things he dismissed as fiction.

She looked up at him from beneath her lashes, the glance tentative, questioning, as if she wondered what he was thinking.

He couldn't let her know.

MARTA PERRY

has written everything from Sunday School curricula to travel articles to magazine stories in more than twenty years of writing, but she feels she's found her writing home in the stories she writes for the Love Inspired lines.

Marta lives in rural Pennsylvania, but she and her husband spend part of each year at their second home in South Carolina. When she's not writing, she's probably visiting her children and her six beautiful grandchildren, traveling, gardening or relaxing with a good book.

Marta loves hearing from readers, and she'll write back with a signed bookmark and/or her brochure of Pennsylvania Dutch recipes. Write to her c/o Steeple Hill Books, 233 Broadway, Suite 1001, New York, NY 10279, e-mail her at marta@martaperry.com, or visit her on the Web at www.martaperry.com.

Heart of the Matter
Marta Perry

Steeple
Hill®

Published by Steeple Hill Books™

STEEPLE HILL BOOKS

Steeple
Hill®

Recycling programs
for this product may
not exist in your area.

ISBN-13: 978-0-373-81455-8

HEART OF THE MATTER

www.SteepleHill.com

Printed in U.S.A.

But seek ye first the kingdom of God,
and his righteousness; and all these things
shall be added unto you.

—Matthew 6:33

This story is dedicated to Pat and Ed Drotos,
my dear sister and brother-in-law.
And, as always, to Brian, with much love.

Chapter One

Amanda Bodine raced around the corner into the newsroom, sure she was late for the staff meeting. She skidded to a halt at the sight of her usually neat, workmanlike desk that now bloomed with a small garden of flowers. Above it floated a balloon bouquet with a streamer that fairly shouted its message. *Happy Birthday.* Her heart plummeted to the pit of her stomach.

She glanced at her watch. Two minutes until the editorial meeting. If she could just get everything out of sight…

"Ms. Bodine." The baritone voice dripped with sarcasm, and she didn't have to turn around to identify the speaker—Ross Lockhart, managing editor of the *Charleston Bugle*. "It seems your personal life is intruding into the office. Again."

"I'm sorry." It wasn't her fault the her large family seemed to take it for granted that they were welcome in her workplace. One noisy visit from two of her cousins had occurred when Lockhart was addressing the staff. He was not amused.

She forced herself to turn and face the man. Drat it, she never had trouble standing up for herself in any other circumstances. Why did her grit turn to jelly in the presence of Ross Lockhart?

Because if you get in his way, he'll mow you down like a blade of grass, her mind promptly responded.

"Get rid of it. Please." The addition of the word didn't do a thing to mitigate the fact that it was an order. "Editorial meeting, people." He raised his voice. "Conference room, now."

A rustle of something that might have been annoyance swept through the newsroom, but no one actually spoke up. No one would. They were all too aware that hotshot journalist Ross Lockhart had been brought in by the *Bugle*'s irascible owner and publisher, Cyrus Mayhew, to ginger things up, as he put it. Lockhart seemed to consider firing people the best way to accomplish that.

Lockhart stalked away in the direction of the conference room before Amanda needed to say another word to him, thank goodness. She should have made sure she'd regained her professional demeanor before coming back to the office from the birthday lunch with her twin sister. Lockhart already seemed to consider her a lightweight in the news business, despite her seven years' experience, and she didn't want to reinforce that impression.

She moved two baskets of roses and daisies to the floor behind her desk and grabbed a notebook to join the exodus from the newsroom.

"Happy birthday, sugar." Jim Redfern, the grizzled city desk editor, threw an arm around her shoulders in a comradely hug. "Too bad you have to spend it in another meeting." His voice lowered. "Sittin' around a table doesn't get a paper out. You'd think the man would realize that."

"He realizes Cyrus expects him to turn us into number one, that's what."

Jim snorted. "Not going to happen in my lifetime."

Nor in hers, probably. Everyone knew that the venerable *Post and Courier,* the oldest newspaper in the South, was Charleston's premier paper. The best the *Bugle* could hope for was to break a surprise story once in a blue moon.

And keep 'em honest, as Cyrus was prone to

say. Everyone who worked at the paper had been treated to his lecture on the importance of competition in the news.

He'd probably like to believe his staff shared that passion.

Entering the high-ceilinged, wood-paneled conference room, Amanda glanced around the table, assessing her colleagues. Cyrus's hope seemed unlikely to be fulfilled. His staffers were either just starting out, hoping this experience would lead to a more important job down the road, or they were old-timers like Jim, put out to pasture by other, more prestigious papers.

She was the only reporter who fit somewhere in the middle, with a year's experience at the Columbia paper, where she'd interned during college, and three years at the *Tampa Tribune* before the lure of the city she loved and the family she loved even more drew her home.

Except for Ross Lockhart, the exception to the rule—smart as a whip, newspaper savvy and ambitious. Above all, ambitious.

Lockhart took his place at the head of the long rectangular table, frowning as usual when he looked at them. He probably found them a pretty unprepossessing bunch compared to the company he'd kept at the Washington, D.C., daily where he'd worked before a public scandal had nearly ruined his career.

She sat up a bit straighter. Maybe they weren't the brightest tools in the tool chest, as her daddy might say, but at least they hadn't fabricated a front-page story, as Lockhart had been accused of doing. And it must have been true, since the paper had made a public apology to the congressman concerned and promptly fired Ross Lockhart.

Lockhart's piercing gray gaze met hers almost as if he'd heard her thoughts, and her throat went dry. Juliet Morrow, the society editor, romantically claimed he had a lean and hungry look, like some crusader of old. The contrast between the steel-gray of his eyes and the true blue-black of his hair, the angular lines of his face, the slash of a mouth—well, maybe she could see what Juliet meant.

But the look he'd turned on her was more that of the wolf eyeing Little Red Riding Hood. She was already sitting near the end of the table. It was impossible to get any farther away from him. Only the obituary writer was lower on the totem pole than she was. She held her breath until his gaze moved on.

He began assigning the stories for the next news cycle. Knowing perfectly well he wouldn't have anything remotely important for her, she fixed her attention on a framed *Bugle* front page that announced VE Day and let her thoughts flicker again to that birthday lunch.

She and her twin were thirty today. Annabel was well and truly launched on the work that was her passion. The others at the meal, more or less the same age, were all either soaring ahead in careers or busy with husband and family. Or both. Only she was entering her thirties stuck in a job where her prospects grew dimmer every time her boss looked her way.

Which he did at that moment. She stiffened. Was there another dog show coming to town that needed her writing talents?

"Bodine." His tone had turned musing. "Seems to me I've heard that name lately. Something connected to the military, wasn't it?"

Her breath caught. Was this the way it would come out—the secret the family struggled to keep in order to protect her grandmother? Right here in the newsroom, in front of everyone, blurted out by a man who had no reason to care who it hurt?

The others at the table were looking at her, their quizzical gazes pressing her for a response. Finally Jim cleared his throat.

"Somethin' about the Coast Guard, maybe?

Bodines tend to serve there." He said the words with the familiar air of someone who knew everything there was to know about old Charleston families…all the things their boss couldn't possibly know.

Lockhart's gaze slashed toward him with an air of clashing swords. Then he shrugged, glancing down at the clipboard in front of him. "Probably so. All right, people, let's get to work."

With a sense of disaster narrowly averted, Amanda followed the others toward the door. Two steps from freedom, Ross Lockhart put out a hand to stop her. "One moment, Ms. Bodine."

She stiffened, turning to face him. Maybe her relief had come too soon.

He leaned back in the chair, eyeing her. She held her breath. If he asked her outright about Ned Bodine, the great-uncle the community had branded a coward, what could she say? She didn't much care what he thought, but if word got out, her grandmother might be hurt.

Finally his focus shifted to the sheaf of papers in front of him. "Mr. Mayhew wants to run a series of articles on the Coast Guard—the functions of the base, its importance to the local economy, maybe some human interest profiles. It seems your family connections might be a help to us in that."

Excitement rippled through her. A real story, finally. "Yes, of course." She was so excited that she nearly tripped over the words. "My father, my brother and my cousins are still on active duty, several stationed right here in Charleston. I'd love to write about—"

He cut her off her enthusiasm with a single cut of his hand. "These will be in-depth pieces. I wasn't suggesting you write them."

Disappointment had a sharp enough edge to make her speak up. "Why not? I'm the most qualified person in the newsroom on the Coast Guard. I did a series when I was at the Tampa paper—"

"Knowing something about a subject doesn't mean you're the best person to write the articles." His tone suggested she should know that. "In fact, I'm taking these on myself. Your role will be to get me access and set up the interviews."

Something anyone with a phone could do, in other words. Naturally he wouldn't let her actually write anything. In Ross Lockhart's eyes, she was nothing but a sweet Southern belle filling in time until marriage by pretending to be a reporter.

Her jaw tightened until she felt it might crack. She could speak her mind, of course. And then she'd go right out the door onto the street behind the other eight people he'd fired.

Finally she swallowed. "I can take care of that."

"Good." He shuffled through his papers, leaving her to wonder if she should go or stay. Then, rising, he held out a half sheet of paper to her. "Get this in for tomorrow's news cycle."

He strode out the door, on to bigger and better things, no doubt. She glanced down at her latest assignment and sucked in an irritated breath.

At least it was a change from a dog show. This time it was a cat show.

Amanda Bodine wasn't quite the person he'd originally thought her. Ross paused at his office door, scanning the newsroom until his gaze lit on her.

Oh, she looked the part, with her chic, glossy brown hair and her trick of looking up at you with those big green eyes from underneath her thick eyelashes. A stereotypical Southern belle, he'd thought—pretty, sweet and brainless. But she wasn't quite that.

The charm was there, yes, and turned on generously for everyone but him. At the moment she was chatting with the kid from the mail room, seeming as interested in him as she'd be if Cyrus Mayhew himself walked up to her.

Everyone's friend—that was Amanda. Even a

crusty old reporter like Jim would pause by her chair, resting his hand on her shoulder long enough to exchange a quip before heading for his desk. Every newsroom had its flirt, and she was theirs.

Amanda was a lightweight, he reminded himself. She didn't belong here. Even if she wasn't quite as shallow as he'd first thought, she didn't have the toughness it took to make a good reporter. Just ask him. He knew exactly how much that cost.

Sooner or later Amanda would take her sweet Southern charm and her big green eyes, marry someone suitable, retreat into her comfortable Charleston lifestyle and produce babies who looked just like her.

No, she didn't belong in a newsroom. He threaded his way purposefully through the desks toward her. But that didn't mean she couldn't be useful. Amanda could give him entrée into a world he'd have trouble penetrating on his own. And that wasn't exactly using her. She was an employee of the paper, after all.

The lie detector inside his mind let out a loud buzz. That was an asset when interviewing the many people who didn't want to tell the truth to a reporter. Not so helpful when it turned on him that way.

Well, okay. He *was* using her. He'd use anyone, try anything, that would get him back to the life where he belonged.

You don't have to trick her. You could tell her about the anonymous tip. Ask for her help.

The voice of his conscience sounded remarkably like that of his grandmother. She'd died when he was a teenager, but the Christian standards she'd set for him still cropped up at inconvenient moments. For an instant he wavered.

Then his resolve hardened. He'd tried being the Boy Scout before, living by his grandmother's ideals, and look where it had gotten him. Clinging to the remnants of his career with his fingernails.

If Cyrus Mayhew hadn't been willing to give him a chance, the only newspaper job he'd have landed was delivering them. In Alaska.

So he'd do what he had to. He frowned. The called-in story tip had been annoyingly vague, as they so often were, but it had promised a scandal, fat and juicy, involving the Coast Guard base and kickbacks paid by local companies for contracts. A big story—the kind of story that, properly handled, could get him back on top again.

And Amanda Bodine, with her Coast Guard family, was just what he needed.

He stalked up to her desk, noting that just the sight of him was enough to send the mail room kid fleeing. Amanda had a bit more self-control, but she clearly didn't welcome his visit, either.

"Ms. Bodine." The balloons were gone from her desk. "Have you set up an initial meeting for me yet?"

"I…um, yes." A faint hint of pink stained her cheeks. "I spoke with my father. He'd be pleased to talk with you."

"Good." He'd done a little digging himself. Talking to Brett Bodine would be starting at the top. He was one of the head honchos at the local Coast Guard base. "When can we meet?"

Her flush deepened, and he watched, fascinated. When was the last time he'd met a woman who could blush?

"Actually, I'm on my way to a family get-together when I leave work. My daddy suggested you come along and have some supper with us. You can talk to him, and my cousins will be there…" Her voice petered out.

"I assume this is a birthday party for you." He lifted an eyebrow, remembering the birthday balloons and flowers. Clearly Amanda had some admirers.

"And my sister, Annabel. We're twins. Since

our birthday is in the summer, we've always had a picnic at the beach." She clamped her mouth shut suddenly, maybe remembering who she was telling.

"It sounds charming."

Her eyes narrowed, as if she suspected sarcasm. "I explained to him that this was business, not social. If you'd rather meet at his office, I can tell him that."

The idea of taking him to a family gathering clearly made her uncomfortable, but it appealed to him. Get people in a casual setting where they felt safe, and they'd often let slip more than they would in a formal interview.

"No, this sounds good," he said briskly. "Give me directions, and I'll be there."

"It's at my grandmother's beach house over on Sullivan's Island." She kept dismay out of her voice, but her mouth had tensed and her hands tightened on the edge of her desk.

"Directions," he said again.

Soft lips pressed together for an instant. "I'll be coming back into the city afterward anyway, if you want to ride over with me instead of trying to find it on your own."

Her brand of Southern courtesy compelled the offer, he supposed, but he was quick to take advantage. A few moments alone in the car with her would give him a chance to get background on the people he'd be meeting.

"Fine," he said promptly. "Are you ready?"

Again the tension showed in her face, but she managed to smile. "Just let me close a few files." She flicked a glance at his shirt and tie. "But you'll want to wear something more casual at the beach."

"I keep a change of clothes in my office." He turned, eager to get on with it. "I'll meet you in the parking lot in fifteen minutes."

He strode toward his office, nodding at the few staffers who ventured to say good-night to him. Most just hurried past, heads down, as if eager to escape his notice. It didn't work. He noticed, just as he'd noticed Amanda's reluctance.

She was both too polite and too worried about her job to argue with him. Even if she had, he'd have been perfectly capable of overrunning her objections.

Amanda didn't want him on her home ground, but that was too bad. Because the Bodines were going to help him get back to *his* native turf, and no other considerations would stand in his way.

Amanda had been treated to a sample of Ross's interview style on the trip over to the island, and she didn't much care for being on the receiving end. She pulled on shorts and T-shirt in the small room under the eaves that the girl cousins always shared at the beach house.

She glanced in the mirror, frowning at the transformation from city professional to island girl. Somehow she felt safer clad in her professional armor.

She pressed her fingertips against the dressing table that still wore the pink-and-white-checked skirt her grandmother had put on it years ago. Not that Miz Callie was a pink and frilly kind of person, but she'd wanted the girl cousins to feel that this room was theirs.

Dealing with Ross in the office was hard enough. Amanda still rankled over his quick dismissal of her ability to write the articles on the Coast Guard. Who was better equipped to write it—someone who'd lived with it her whole life or an outsider who didn't have a clue?

She wrinkled her nose at the image in the mirror. Ross had the answer to that, and he was the boss. He'd decided that her family was his way into the story, and if his aggressive, almost abrasive questioning in the car had been a sample of his style, they were in for some rough waters.

She headed for the stairs, the comparison lightening her mood. Daddy was used to rough waters. He could handle the likes of Ross with one hand tied behind his back.

And speaking of handling him, she'd left her boss alone with her grandmother. Goodness only knows what they were making of each other.

She usually skipped down the stairs at the beach house because of the sheer joy of being there. Now she hurried for fear of what Miz Callie might be saying. Catching Ross's gaze on her, she slowed to a more sedate pace as she reached the living room.

He was sitting in the shabby, over-stuffed chair near the wall of windows that faced the beach and the ocean. Her heart clutched. That had been Granddad's special seat after his first stroke had stolen away most of his mobility. He'd never tired of looking out at the sea.

"Is my grandmother takin' good care of you?" The tall glass of sweet tea at his elbow looked untouched.

"She is. She had to run back to the kitchen to deal with something." As if becoming aware of the glass, he lifted it and touched it to his lips.

She couldn't help but grin. "Obviously you aren't used to iced tea that's sweet enough to make your back teeth ache. Come on. We'll find the others. Someone will have brought a cooler of soda."

He put the sweet tea down quickly and stood, his gaze sweeping over her. She usually felt he didn't see her at all. This gaze was far more personal. Too much so.

Her chin lifted. "Something wrong?" She edged the words with ice.

"No." He made an instinctive move back. "You just look different. From the office, that is."

"We're not in the office," she pointed out. If she could make him feel a tad uncomfortable, so much the better. She needed to keep a professional distance between them, no matter where they were.

"We're not," he agreed. His fingers brushed her bare arm, and the unexpected familiarity of the gesture set her nerve endings tingling.

He nodded toward the kitchen. "We were going in search of a soda," he reminded her.

"Right, yes." She took a breath. She would not let the man dismantle her confidence in herself. "This way."

But as she started for the kitchen, he stopped her with another touch. This time his hand lingered on her wrist, warming the skin. "In this setting, it's going to sound odd if you call me Mr.

Lockhart. Let's switch to first names. Amanda," he added, smiling.

She nodded. What could she do but agree? But she'd been right. His smile really did make him look like the Big Bad Wolf.

She led the way into the kitchen, aware of him hard on her heels.

The kitchen was a scene of contained chaos, as it always was when the whole family gathered at the beach house. Her mamma and one of her aunts talked a mile a minute while they chopped veggies for a salad, her sister Annabel and cousin Georgia arranged nibbles on a huge tray, and Miz Callie, swathed in an apron that nearly swallowed her five-foot-nothing figure, peered anxiously at the contents of a huge kettle—pulled pork barbecue, judging by the aroma.

"Did y'all meet my boss, Ross Lockhart?"

"We introduced ourselves, sugar." Mamma stopped chopping long enough to plant a kiss on her cheek. "You comin' to help us?"

Miz Callie clattered the lid back onto the pot. "She'd best introduce her friend to the men first. I don't suppose he wants to be stuck in the kitchen."

"I'm afraid my cooking skills wouldn't be up to your standards, Mrs. Bodine," Ross said quickly. "It smells way too good in here."

Miz Callie dimpled up at him, always charmed by a compliment to her cooking. "The proof is in the eating, you know. You let Amanda get you settled with someone to talk to, and later on we'll get better acquainted."

"I'll look forward to it."

Amanda gave him a sharp glance, ready to do battle if he was being condescending to her grandmother. But his expression had actually softened, and his head was tilted deferentially toward Miz Callie.

Well. So something could pierce that abrasive shield he wore. That was a surprise.

Still, it would be just as well to keep him from any lengthy tête-à-têtes with her grandmother. Miz Callie was still obsessed with that old scandal about her husband's brother and they surely didn't need to let Ross Lockhart in on the skeleton in the Bodine family closet.

"This way." She put a hand on the glass door and slid it back. "Anybody who's not in the kitchen is probably down on the beach."

Ross followed her onto the deck that ran the length of the house and paused, one hand on the railing. "Beautiful view."

"It is that." She lifted her face to the breeze that freshened the hot summer air. "On a clear day you feel as if you can see all the way across the Atlantic."

He turned his back on the ocean to have a look at the beach house sprawled comfortably on the dunes, its tan shingles blending into sand and sea oats. "Has your family had the place long?" The speculative note in his voice suggested he was estimating the cost.

"For generations." She clipped off the words. They couldn't afford to build a house on the beach at today's prices, but that was none of Ross Lockhart's business. "My great-grandfather bought this piece of property back when there was no bridge to the mainland and nothing much on the island but Fort Moultrie and a few fishing shacks."

"Very nice." He glanced toward the kitchen, and she realized he was looking at Miz Callie with that softened glance. "Did I understand your grandmother lives here year-round?"

"That's her plan. The family's been trying to talk her out of it, but once Miz Callie makes up her mind, you may as well save your breath to cool your porridge, as she'd say."

His lips curved. "I had a grandmother like that, too. A force to be reckoned with."

"Had?" She reacted automatically to the past tense.

"She died when I was a teenager." He turned to her, closer than she'd realized. Her breath hitched in her throat. "You're lucky to have your grandmother still. Very lucky."

The intensity in his low voice set up an answering vibration in her. For a moment they seemed linked by that shared emotion.

Then she caught herself and took a careful step back. *This is your boss, remember? You don't even like him.*

But she couldn't deny that, just for a moment, he'd shown her a side of himself that she'd liked very much.

Chapter Two

The long living room of the beach house overflowed with Bodines. Ross balanced a plate of chocolate caramel cake on his lap, surveying them from a seat in the corner.

Clearly they were a prolific bunch. He'd finally straightened it out that the grandmother, Miz Callie, as they called her, had three sons. Each of them had produced several children to swell the brood.

Judging by all the laughter and hugging they were a close family, almost claustrophobically so. Who could imagine having a party with this many people—all of them related?

He certainly couldn't. His family had consisted of his parents, Gran and himself. That was it. His father had said more than once that having no siblings was a distinct advantage for a politician—they couldn't embarrass you.

That had been the creed by which he'd been raised. *Don't do anything to embarrass your father.*

And he hadn't, not even slightly, for all those years, until that final, spectacular event. His fingers tightened on the dessert plate, and he forced them to relax.

Forget his family. Forget his past mistakes. The thing to do now was to concentrate on the job at hand. If he could isolate Amanda's father for a quiet chat…

Miz Callie, a cup of coffee in her hand, headed in his direction. Tiny, probably not much over five feet, she was trim and lively, with a halo of white hair and blue eyes that hadn't faded with age. She sat down next to him.

"How's the cake? Can I get you anything else?"

"The cake is wonderful." He took a bite, realizing that the compliment was true. He'd been so busy thinking about the job that he hadn't even tasted it. "Thank you, Mrs. Bodine."

"Call me Miz Callie." She patted his arm. "Everyone does. We're just so glad to meet you at last. Amanda talks about you often."

He noticed she didn't specify what Amanda said. That wouldn't be polite. He could imagine that Amanda had broadcast her opinion of him to her clan.

"You have quite a family. I'm not sure I have them all straight yet. Several in the Coast Guard, I understand." Mrs. Bodine—Miz Callie, rather—might have some insights he could tap.

"That's a family tradition," she said absently. Her attention was on Amanda and her sister as they cut slices of cake. "Devil's food cake with caramel icing is Amanda and Annabel's favorite, so we always have it for their birthday. Funny that they like the same thing, because they're different as can be in other ways."

If this were an interview, he could get her back onto the subject of the Coast Guard with a direct question. In polite conversation, it wasn't so easy.

"They look nearly identical." Same honey-brown hair, same deep green eyes, same slim, lithe figures. They were striking, seen together.

"Identical in looks, but not in temperament." Miz Callie's blue eyes crinkled. "Amanda is fifteen minutes older, and she's always been the big sister, the high achiever. And always trying to best her two older brothers, too."

He could tell the twins apart not by appearance so much as by body language and expression.

Amanda was livelier, teasing and being teased, laughing easily.

"Annabel seems a little quieter."

"She goes her own way," Miz Callie said. "She always has. Never especially bothered by what everyone else is doing."

"Everyone else in this case being family?"

"I s'pose so." She twinkled at him. "There's quite a tribe of us, as you can see. And all the cousins are so close in age, too. Still, I guess family gatherings are all pretty much alike everywhere."

He nodded in agreement, although nothing could be further from the truth when it came to comparing this noisy crowd to his family. "They all seem very close."

That was not entirely a compliment, at least not in his mind. He wouldn't care to have this many people feeling they had a right to tell him what to do.

"Close." She repeated the word, but her tone gave it a different meaning. "I wish…"

Alerted, he studied her face. There was something there—some worry or concern evident in the clouding of those clear eyes, the tension in the fine lines around her lips.

"You wish…" he prompted.

She seemed to come back from a distance, or

maybe from thoughts she didn't welcome. She shook her head. "Goodness, I'm forgetting why you're here. You want to talk to the boys about the Coast Guard, and here I'm yammering on about everything else."

She was out of her chair before he could move. "Adam, come on over here and talk to Ross. He's wantin' to write something about the service."

Adam…Bodine, he supposed, they were all Bodines, came in obedience to his grandmother's hail.

"Sure thing, Miz Callie." He bent to plant a kiss on her cheek. "But I'll just bet he'd rather talk to you."

She gave him a playful swat and scurried off before Ross could do anything more than rise from his chair. Since Adam didn't take the empty seat, he remained standing, putting them eye to eye.

Tall, muscular, with an open, friendly smile— the man had been introduced to him, probably, but he couldn't for the life of him remember if this was Amanda's brother or cousin.

Adam grinned, almost as if he interpreted the thought. "Adam Bodine," he prompted. "Amanda's cousin. That's my sister, Georgia, pouring out the coffee. My daddy's the one standing next to Amanda's daddy. It's tough to sort us all out."

"I'm usually pretty good with names, but—"

"But we're all Bodines," Adam said, finishing for him. "Amanda tells us you're fixing to do some articles for the newspaper about the service."

"The Coast Guard seems important to the community, so it's a good subject for a series of articles." That bit ran smoothly off his tongue. "What made so many of you decide on that for a career?"

"Ask each of us, you'd get a different reason." Adam nodded toward one of the laughing group clustered around the twins. "My cousin Win, now, he's a rescue swimmer. He always was a daredevil, so jumping out of a chopper feels normal to him. He'd say he's in it for the excitement. Me, I couldn't imagine a life that didn't involve being on the water. My daddy was the same." He paused, as if he looked deeper at the question. "Bottom line is serving our country, I guess."

"Patriotism." He tried not to let cynicism leak into his voice. Maybe he was jaundiced. He'd seen his father wave the flag too many times out of political expediency.

Adam's gaze met his. "That's somethin' we take kind of serious around here. Charleston's been a military town since the Revolution, and we have more military retirees here than most any place in the country our size."

"All the more reason to highlight what you do and the effect it has on the community," he said quickly, not wanting to get on the wrong side of the man. "Financially, for instance. I'm sure many companies in Charleston benefit from having the station here. It has to pump money into the local economy."

And into someone's pocket, if his informant was right.

"Sure, I guess so. My uncle Brett's the one you should talk to about that, though." He beckoned to Amanda's father, who veered in their direction. "Me, I just know about cutters and patrol boats."

Brett Bodine was probably in his early fifties, with a square, bluff face and a firm manner. He nodded, a little stiffly, and Ross wondered again what Amanda had been telling her family about her boss.

"Ross was just asking me about somethin' I figured you could answer better, Uncle Brett."

"What's that?" The man was measuring him with his gaze, and it looked as if he wasn't impressed with what he saw.

"He's wanting to know about the base doing business with local merchants, that kind of thing."

Adam took a step back, as if leaving the field to his uncle.

Ross barely noticed. All his attention was on Brett Bodine. In the instant Adam had said those words, the man had reacted...a sudden tension in the erect figure, a flicker of wariness in the eyes, an involuntary twitch in the jaw.

Barely perceptible, unless you were looking. Unless your instincts were those of a trained interviewer, alert for the signs that you'd hit pay dirt.

Brett Bodine recovered quickly, Ross would say that for him. He'd managed a fairly pleasant smile in a matter of seconds.

"I'll put you in touch with our information officer," he said briskly. "She'll be glad to answer your questions."

She'd be glad to give Ross the canned speech, in other words. "In order to do a series of in-depth articles, I need to talk to the people who are actually involved in the work. Amanda thought you could help me with that."

The man's face tightened, as if he didn't like the reminder that Ross was his daughter's employer. "Our information office will—"

"Daddy." Amanda stood next to them, and they'd been so intent on their battle of wills that neither of them had noticed her. "I told you how important this is. You're not going to fob us off on someone else, are you?"

Us, she'd said. Apparently Amanda considered them a team. Well, if that's what it took to get him what he wanted, so be it.

Bodine's deeply tanned face reddened slightly in a flare of temper, but it eased when he looked at his daughter. He shrugged, seeming to give in to the inevitable.

"I guess not," he said. "We'll set it up for you to come in and talk in the next couple of days."

The words sounded right, but again, Ross read the body language, and it said exactly the opposite. Something was going on—something that Brett Bodine obviously knew about.

And something that, just as clearly, Amanda didn't.

For probably the first time in her life, Amanda was eager to leave the beach house. The party had been lovely, but she couldn't control the stress she felt at having her boss there.

That was all it was. Surely she'd been imagining the tension she'd thought existed between Daddy and Ross. They didn't even know each other. What did they have to be at odds about?

She popped her head in the kitchen door,

looking for Miz Callie to say her goodbyes and thanks. Her grandmother probably shouldn't still be putting on birthday parties for the family, but no one had enough nerve to tell her so.

The kitchen was empty, the dishwasher humming, but before she could turn away, Miz Callie came in from the deck.

"There's the birthday girl. Come here, sugar, and let me give you a birthday kiss."

"And one to grow on," Amanda said, smiling, and kissed her grandmother's soft cheek. For a moment she stood, Miz Callie's comforting arms wrapped around her, and unexpected tears welled in her eyes.

She couldn't think of her vibrant, energetic grandmother, the rock of the family, as growing old. It was too soon for that.

She blinked back the tears, knowing what had put that thought into her mind. For months Miz Callie had been obsessed with the idea of righting an old wrong. She kept saying that it must be done before she died; a constant reminder that their precious grandmother might not have too many years left hurt.

Miz Callie drew back and patted her cheek. "Amanda, honey, have you found out anything more about Ned?"

And there it was—the albatross that seemed to be hanging 'round all their necks these days. Ned Bodine, Granddad's older brother. They'd none of them even known him, except Miz Callie. He'd left long ago, running off in 1942, never in touch with the family again. Every old-timer in the county believed he'd run out of cowardice, afraid to fight in the war.

Amanda's cousin Georgia, the first one Miz Callie had trusted with her quest, had found out that what everyone believed wasn't true. Instead, after a sad love story and a rift with his father, Ned had left the island to enlist under a false name.

And there the story ended, as far as they'd been able to discover. How could you trace an anonymous man who could have gone anywhere, used any name?

Miz Callie's eyes grew suspiciously bright, and she patted Amanda's cheek again, her hand gentle. "It's all right, darlin'. You don't need to say it. I guess it's too much to hope for after all this time."

Pain twisted her heart. "We won't give up. There must be something else I can try."

She glanced toward the deck where her cousin Georgia stood with her fiancé's arm around her waist. Matt's little girl, Lindsay, leaned against

Georgia trustingly. Lucky Georgia. She'd not only found the first clues to what had happened to Ned—she'd found love in the process.

Miz Callie shook her head slowly. "Maybe it's time to give up on learning anything more. The nature preserve is nearly ready to go. Maybe I'd best just make the announcement and be done with it."

"But Miz Callie, the scandal…" She bit her lip. The family might be satisfied that Ned hadn't been a coward, but they didn't have the proof that would convince anyone else. Plenty of folks would be unhappy at Miz Callie's plan to dedicate the nature preserve she planned for a small barrier island to a man they considered a disgrace to Charleston's proud patriotic tradition. She had a vision of scores of military veterans marching down Meeting Street in protest. Army, Navy, Air Force, Marines, Coast Guard—they'd all had a presence here at one time or another.

"I reckon we can live down a scandal if we have to." Miz Callie wiped away a tear with the back of her hand. "I just want to get this done."

"I know. But a little more time won't hurt, will it?"

Please. They'd present a brave face to the world if it came to that. The family was agreed.

But Miz Callie would be so hurt if folks she'd known all her life turned against her.

A fierce love burned in Amanda. She couldn't let that happen.

"I'll work on it. I promise." She was the reporter in the family, after all. Finding out things was her job. At least it was more important than covering pet shows. "You'll wait, right?" She looked pleadingly at her grandmother.

Miz Callie nodded. "I will. Don't worry so much, darlin'. God will show us the way."

She let out a relieved breath. She believed God would guide them, but she couldn't help wanting to chart this course herself. "Good. I'll…"

The sound of movement behind her stopped her words. She turned. Ross stood in the doorway. How long had he been there?

"I don't want to take you away from your party, but I do need to get back to the office."

"That's all right," she said quickly. "I'll just get my things."

Had he heard her conversation with Miz Callie or hadn't he? It worried at her as she gathered her things. She had to say goodbye to everyone, had to endure all the teasing about being a year older and exchange a special hug with Annabel, aware all the time that her boss stood waiting.

Finally, she got out the door, walking to the car with Ross on her heels.

The air between them sizzled with more than the summer heat as she started the car and turned the air-conditioning on high. And that was her answer. He'd heard something of what Miz Callie said. She wasn't sure how she knew, but she did. It was just there, in his concentrated expression.

They passed the island's park, the small collection of shops and restaurants, the old Gullah cemetery. Finally, as they approached the drawbridge that would take them off the island, she could stand it no longer.

"You heard what my grandmother said, didn't you?"

If that sounded like an accusation—well, she guessed it was. She spared a fleeting thought for her fired colleagues. Maybe she'd soon be joining them.

Silence for a moment. She saw the movement of his head at the edge of her vision as he turned to look at her.

"I wasn't eavesdropping, if that's what you're implying." His tone was surprisingly even. "I realized that your grandmother was upset, so I didn't come in. I'm not in the habit of listening in on the worries of elderly ladies."

She wasn't sure that she believed him. Still—

"You'd best not let her hear you call her elderly." She managed an apologetic smile. "I'm sorry. I hate it when she gets upset."

It was none of his business what Miz Callie had been upset about. Amanda had the sudden sense that the family skeleton had grown to an unmanageable size and was about to burst from its closet.

"You have a good heart." He sounded almost surprised.

"I love her," she said. "I'm sure you felt the same about your grandmother."

He nodded, staring out the window at the marsh grasses and pluff mud.

There didn't seem anywhere else to go with that conversation. She cleared her throat. "I hope meeting my people was helpful to you. For the articles, I mean."

"Very. You'll set up that appointment with your father as soon as possible."

"Right." When he didn't respond, she glanced at him. "Don't you want to talk to anyone else? My cousin Win is a rescue swimmer."

She held out the prospect enticingly. Win, an outgoing charmer, would be delighted to be interviewed, and surely that would be more interesting to readers than Daddy's desk job.

"What?" Her question seemed to have recalled Ross from some deep thought. "Yes, I suppose. I'll think about it and let you know."

Odd. Not her business, she guessed, how he approached the series of articles he said he was writing, but odd all the same.

She stole a sideways glance at him. His lean face seemed closed against the world, his eyes hooded and secretive.

Why? What made him so forbidding? The professional scandal they'd all heard of, or something more?

She gave herself a mental shake. This was the man who kept the entire news staff dangling over the abyss of unemployment. Maybe she felt a bit easier in his presence since this little expedition, but that didn't mean she knew him.

Or that she could trust him any farther than she could throw him.

He was going to have to tread carefully with Amanda, Ross decided. Something had made her suspicious of him after that family party the previous day.

He stood back to let the high school student intern precede him into the newsroom, assessing the young woman as he did. Cyrus Mayhew had chosen the recipient of his journalism internship on the basis of her writing, not her personality.

C. J. Dillon was bright, no doubt about that. She was also edgy and more than a little wary.

Suspicious, like Amanda.

The new intern had no reason for her suspicion, other than maybe the natural caution of a young black woman from a tough inner-city school toward the establishment, represented at the moment by him.

Amanda, on the other hand...well, maybe she did have just cause. He'd told the truth when he said he'd stopped outside the kitchen because he'd realized her grandmother was upset. He'd just neglected to mention that he'd heard the word *scandal* used in relation to her family. Or that all his instincts had gone on alert.

If he wanted to find out what scandal in the Bodine family would leave the grandmother in tears, he'd better find a way to mend fences with Amanda.

Assigning the student intern to her might disarm her. From what he'd seen of Amanda's relationship with everyone from the mail room kid to the cleaning crew, taking in strays was second nature to her.

"This way." He moved ahead of C.J. to lead her

through the maze of desks in the newsroom. A few cautious glances slid their way. C.J. couldn't know that the looks were aimed at him, not her.

All right, so his staff didn't trust him. That was fine with him. He was here to turn this newspaper around, not make friends. He didn't need any more so-called friends who waited with a sharpened knife for him to make a slip.

Amanda's desk was at the far end of the row. Focused on her computer, a pair of glasses sliding down her nose, she didn't see them coming. She wore her usual version of business casual—well-cut tan slacks, a silky turquoise shirt, a slim gold chain around her neck.

That was a bit different from the way she'd looked at the beach house in an old pair of shorts and a Fort Moultrie T-shirt. He let his mind stray to the image. That had definitely been casual, to say nothing of showing off a pair of slim, tanned legs and a figure that would make any man look twice.

He yanked his unruly thoughts back to business. Amanda's only usefulness to him was the opening she provided to the Coast Guard base. And given that tantalizing mention of scandal, to the Bodine family in particular.

He stopped a few feet from her desk, feeling the need for a little distance between them.

"Ms. Bodine." *Amanda*, he thought, but didn't say.

Her gaze jerked away from the computer screen. The startled look she turned on him softened into a smile when she saw that he wasn't alone. No, the smile wouldn't be for him.

"This is C. J. Dillon. C.J., I'd like you to meet one of our reporters, Amanda Bodine."

"Hi, C.J. It's nice to meet you." Amanda held out her hand. After a moment, the young woman took it gingerly.

"C.J. is the winner of the journalism competition Mr. Mayhew set up in the local schools." The contest had been another of Cyrus's bright ideas for drawing attention to the *Bugle*, and all the staff should certainly be aware of it.

"That's great. Congratulations." She focused on C.J. "What did you win?"

Obviously the staff, or at least this member of it, hadn't kept up-to-date. His decision was even more appropriate, then.

"C.J. has received a six-week internship with the newspaper. A chance to find out if journalism is the right career for her, as Mr. Mayhew said in his editorial about the competition."

Which you should have read. The words were

unspoken, but Amanda no doubt caught his meaning, since her lips tightened.

"You'll be happy to know I've decided to assign C.J. to work with you for the duration. You're going to be her mentor."

"I see." A momentary pause as Amanda turned to the young woman, and then came the smile that resembled the sun coming up over the ocean— the one she had yet to turn on him. "That's great, C.J. I look forward to working with you."

The ironic thing was that she probably did. For him, this brainstorm of Cyrus's was nothing but a nuisance. He had no particular desire to have a high school kid wandering around his newsroom.

Still, paired with Amanda, she couldn't do much harm. And if Amanda could persuade her that skintight jeans and a skimpy top weren't appropriate professional apparel, so much the better.

"Don't I have anything to say about who I work with?" The kid turned a belligerent frown on him. "I don't want to run around town covering stuff like boat parades and charity races. That's all she does."

He'd been so intent upon ridding himself of the problem that he was actually surprised when the kid spoke up. Irritation edged along his nerves. She was lucky to be here. Still, she'd obviously done her homework and paid attention to bylines.

"C.J., that's how everyone starts out," Amanda said quickly, as if to block out his response. Maybe she sensed his annoyance. "You're lucky you weren't assigned to the obit desk. This is much better than writing obituaries, believe me."

C.J. didn't noticeably soften. "Not much," she muttered.

"Hey, we do interesting stories. In fact, this afternoon we're heading down to Coast Guard Base Charleston for an interview. You'll have a chance to see the inside workings of the place."

"We?" He stressed the word. Taking Amanda along on interviews hadn't been part of his plan.

Amanda's eyebrows lifted. "My father is expecting us at three-thirty today. I hope that works for you."

He was tempted to make it clear that he didn't need or want her company. But if he did, that could put paid to any more help on her part. He might need her goodwill to gain future access.

"Fine." He tried to look as if he welcomed her company. "I'll see you then."

He turned away, startled to realize that on at least one level, he did.

Chapter Three

Amanda didn't know whether she was more relieved or surprised that Ross didn't fight her on the visit to Coast Guard Base Charleston, but he'd headed back to his office without further comment. Maybe he was beginning to see that she had something to offer. If this worked out well, maybe he'd…

She looked at C.J., and she came back to earth with a thump. Ross hadn't changed his mind about her. He just hadn't wanted to get into a hassle in front of the new intern.

No, that didn't sound like Ross. He didn't mind coming off dictatorial, no matter who was listening.

Thinking of him had brought a frown to her face. Amanda replaced it with a smile for C.J.

Although, come to think of it, she wasn't exactly feeling warm toward the young woman. What had she meant by her outspoken distaste for working with Amanda?

She nodded toward a chair at the vacant desk next to hers—vacant since Ross had decided that its occupant was expendable. "Pull that seat over, so we can talk."

Wearing a sullen expression, C.J. rolled the chair to Amanda's desk and plopped into it, folding her arms.

Amanda had to hide a grin. C.J.'s body language was eloquent. Still, she'd have to learn that she couldn't call the shots at this point in her career. Any more than Amanda could.

"I suppose you've been working on your school newspaper," she ventured, wondering what the key would be to opening up this abrasive personality.

C.J.'s lips pressed together. After a moment, she shook her head. "Have to be a teacher's little pet for that, don't you? Anyway, I'm not gonna write stupid stories about poster contests and decorating the gym. I want to write about important things. That's why I entered the contest."

That hit a little too close to home. "Sounds like we have something in common then," she said briskly. "We both want to write more challenging subjects." She'd never really regretted retuning home, but the truth was that with the paper's already well-established staff, it was tough to move up. Especially when the new editor refused to believe she could write.

C.J. glowered at her for another moment, and then she shrugged.

Amanda resisted the desire to shake her. Working with this kid might be an exercise in suppressing emotions.

"Okay, then." Might as well go on the offensive, since nothing else seemed effective. "How did you know what kind of articles I write?"

Another shrug. "I know what everyone who works for the paper writes. It's my thing, isn't it?"

So she'd put time and effort into this chance at success. Did she even realize that her attitude was working against her? With a more accommodating spirit and some advice on what to wear, C.J. could come out of this on the road to success.

Dismayed, Amanda recognized her crusading spirit rising. It was the same irresistible urge that led her to one lame duck after another, always convinced that somehow she could help them.

And she had, more often than not. Her brothers

insisted that her victims, as they called them, responded because that was the only way they could get rid of her, but she didn't buy that. That hapless Bangladeshi student at College of Charleston would have been sent home before he finished his degree if not for her organizing his fight to stay. And the article she'd written about endangered sea turtle nests had helped move along a new lighting ordinance.

Given C.J.'s attitude toward her, it was unlikely that the young woman would be one of her success stories. Still, she had to try.

"If you really mean to make journalism your career, an internship is a great place to start, especially getting one while you're still in high school. I didn't have one until the summer between my junior and senior years of college."

C.J.'s eyes betrayed a faint spark of interest. "Where did you go?"

"University of South Carolina. I interned at the Columbia paper that summer. Writing obits," she added, just in case C.J. had missed that part. "What schools are you looking at?"

C.J.'s dark eyes studied the floor. "Can't afford USC, that's for sure. Maybe I can work and take classes at Trident," she said, naming the community college.

Amanda opened her mouth to encourage her and closed it again. She didn't know what kind of grades C.J. had, or what her home situation was. It would be wrong for her to hold out hope without more information.

She hadn't ever had to doubt that she'd be able to attend any college she could get into. Her parents had put a high priority on education for their four kids, no matter what they might have to sacrifice. C.J. might not be so lucky.

"How long you been here, anyway?" C.J. glanced around the newsroom, gaze lingering on Jim for a moment. As well-informed as she seemed, she undoubtedly knew that he wrote the kinds of stories Amanda could only dream about.

"Three years." She'd had her reasons for coming home, good ones, but maybe it hadn't turned out to be the smartest career path.

She was closing in on her ten-year college reunion, and still near the bottom of the journalism ladder, writing stories no one read but the people immediately involved.

C.J. eyed her. "If I had the edge you have, I'd sure be doing better by the time I got to be your age."

Was C.J. the voice of her conscience, sent to remind her that it was time she accomplished something worthwhile? Or just an obnoxious kid who would alienate everyone who might be willing to help her?

She slapped one hand down on her desk, making the silver-framed photo of her family tremble. "Now you look." She put some fire into her voice. "This internship can be the chance of a lifetime for you, but not if you go into it determined to annoy everyone you meet. You may be bright and talented, but so are a lot of other people. Talent won't get you anywhere without hard work and plenty of goodwill. Got that?"

She waited for the kid to flare up at her. C.J. pressed her lips together for a long moment. Finally she nodded. "Yes, ma'am," she muttered.

Well, that was progress of a sort. Maybe C.J. had what it took to get something from this experience. She prayed so.

As for C.J.'s opinion of her—there wasn't much she could do to change that, because like it or not, it was probably true.

Ross's finger hovered over the reply icon for a moment, then moved to delete. Finally he just closed the e-mail. He'd consider later what, if anything, he should say to his mother.

How long had it been since she'd been in touch with him? A month, at least. And that previous message had been much the same as this latest one—an impersonal recitation of his parents' busy lives. A perfunctory question as to how he was doing. A quick sign-off.

As for his father…well, he hadn't heard from his father since he left D.C. The last thing Congressman Willard Lockhart needed was a son who'd made the front page in the headline rather than the byline.

"Ross? Do you have a minute?"

He swung his chair around and rose, startled at the sight of the *Bugle*'s owner, Cyrus Mayhew. "Of course. What is it?"

"Nothin' much." Cyrus wandered in, moving aimlessly around the office.

Ross felt his hands tighten and deliberately relaxed them. When Cyrus got aimless and folksy, it was a sure sign there was something on his mind. He might not know a lot about his employer yet, but he did know that.

Cyrus picked up a paperweight and balanced it on his palm, then put it back. He moved to the window, walked back to the desk. Peered at Ross, blue eyes sharp beneath bushy white brows. Someone had compared Cyrus to Mark Twain, and he seemed to deliberately cultivate the similarity.

The tension crawled along Ross's skin again,

refusing to be dispelled. "Something special you wanted, sir?"

"Just wondering if you got that intern settled. Seemed like a nice youngster—maybe a little rough around the edges, though."

That was an understatement. "I assigned her to work with Amanda Bodine."

"Good, good. Amanda will take her under her wing. Might be a good role model for her."

She would, but somehow he didn't think that was all that was on Cyrus's mind today.

"Was there anything else?" he prompted.

"Well, now, I wondered what's going on with that tip we discussed. Anything in it?"

"It's too soon to tell."

Maybe he'd have been better off to keep that tip to himself. Was Cyrus really the elderly gadfly, intent on keeping the establishment honest? Or would he, like so many others, sell anyone out for a big story?

His stomach clenched. The face of his former mentor and boss flickered through his mind, and he forced it away. It didn't pay to think about the mentor who'd sacked him without listening to explanations, or the friend who'd stabbed him in the back without a second thought.

"But you're lookin' into it, aren't you, son?"

"I'm following up on everything we have, which isn't much. An anonymous call from someone who said businessmen were paying graft to get contracts at the Coast Guard base. A couple of anonymous letters saying the same thing, but giving no other details."

Cyrus nodded, musing, absently patting the round belly he was supposed to be dieting away. "We need to get on the inside, that's what we need."

"I'm working on that now, sir. I have an appointment with someone down at the base this afternoon."

Maybe it was best not to mention who. And even more important not to mention that tantalizing fragment he'd overheard from Amanda's grandmother.

"Good, good. Keep at it." Cyrus rubbed his palms together, as if he were already looking at a front-page spread. "We can't afford to let this slip through our fingers. This is the real deal—I can feel it."

"I hope so." For more reasons than one.

Like Cyrus, he wanted a big story for the *Bugle*, but even more, he wanted one for himself. He wanted to erase the pain and humiliation of the past year.

Irrational. No one could erase the past.

But one great job of investigative reporting could get his life back again. The need burned in him. To go back to the life he was born for, to dig into important stories, to feel he was making a difference in the world.

This was the best chance he'd had since he'd come to the *Bugle*. As Cyrus said, he couldn't let it slip between his fingers.

Amanda stood outside the redbrick building on Tradd Street that was headquarters of Coast Guard Base Charleston, waiting with C.J. while Ross parked the car. She was beginning to wish she'd had a chance to talk to the intern about proper professional clothing before taking her out on this initial assignment.

Ross came around the corner of the building, and before he could reach them C.J. nudged her. "So, you and the boss—are you together?"

"Together?" For a moment her mind was a blank. Then she realized the implication and felt a flush rising in her cheeks. "No, certainly not. What would make you think that?"

C.J. shrugged. "Dunno. Vibes, I guess. I'm pretty good at reading them."

"Not this time." Her fingers tightened on the strap of her bag. What on earth had led the kid to that conclusion? Were people talking, just because she'd taken him to the beach house?

Well, wouldn't they? The inner voice teased her. *You'd talk, if it were anyone else.*

That should have occurred to her. The newsroom was a hotbed of gossip, mostly false. She could only hope Ross hadn't gotten wind of it.

"Our relationship is strictly professional," she added. Obviously she'd have to make that clear to C.J. and to the newsroom in general. To say nothing of herself.

He joined them, and that increased awareness made her feel stiff and unnatural. She nodded toward the door. "Shall we go in?"

Fortunately she knew the petty officer on duty at the desk. That would make it simpler to ask a favor.

"Hey, Amanda." Kelly Ryan's smile included all of them. "You're expected. Go on up." She thrust visitor badges across to them.

"Is anyone free to take our intern on a tour while we're in with my father?" Sensing a rebellious comment forming on C.J.'s lips, she went on quickly. "I'd like her to gather background color for the articles we're doing. Okay?"

C.J. subsided.

"Sure thing. I'll handle it." Kelly waved them toward the stairs.

They headed up, leaving C.J. behind with Kelly, and she was still too aware of Ross, following on her heels. Drat the kid, anyway. Why did C.J. have to suggest something like that? It wasn't as if she didn't feel awkward enough around Ross already.

Ross touched her elbow as they reached the office. "One thing before we go in. This is my interview, remember."

"How could I forget?" She just managed not to snap the words. She'd like to blame C.J., but the annoyance she felt wasn't entirely due to the intern's mistaken impression.

She shot a sideways glance at Ross and recognized what she felt emanating from him. Tension. A kind of edgy eagerness that she didn't understand. What was going on with him?

They walked into the office. Her father, imposing in his blue dress uniform, rose from behind his desk to greet them.

Under the cover of the greetings and light conversation, she sought for calm.

I don't know what's going on, Father. I'm not sure what Ross wants, but it must be something beyond what he's told me. Please, guide me now.

Her gaze, skittering around the room as the two men fenced with verbal politeness, landed on the framed photo on her father's desk. The family, taken at the beach on their Christmas Day walk last year. It was the same photo she had on her desk. Somehow the sight of those smiling faces seemed to settle her.

She focused her attention on Ross. He was asking a series of what seemed to be routine, even perfunctory, questions about her father's work and the function of the base.

"The Coast Guard is now under the Department of Homeland Security," her father said, clearly not sure Ross knew anything about the service. "Our jobs include maritime safety. Most people think of that first, the rescue work. But there's also security, preventing trafficking of drugs, contrabands, illegal immigrants. We protect the public, the environment and U.S. economic and security interests in any maritime region, including lakes and rivers."

This was her father at his most formal. He could be telling Ross some of the kinds of stories she'd heard over the dinner table since she was a kid—exciting rescues, chemical spills prevented, smugglers caught. Why was he being so stiff?

A notebook rested on Ross's knee, but he wasn't bothering to write down the answers Daddy gave. Maybe he was just absorbing background information. She often worked that way, too, not bothering to write down information she could easily verify later with a press kit.

But that didn't account for the level of tension she felt in the room—tension that didn't come solely from Ross. Her father's already square jaw seemed squarer than ever, and his lips tightened at a routine question.

"I don't see why you need information on our local contractors." He bit the words off sharply.

"We'd like to show how much money the base brings into the local economy." Ross's explanation sounded smooth.

Too smooth. She'd already sampled his interview style, and this wasn't it. As for her father…

Ordinarily when Daddy looked the way he did at the moment, he was on the verge of an explosion. No one had ever accused Brett Bodine of being patient in the face of aggravation.

There was no doubt in her mind that he found Ross's questions annoying. But why? They seemed innocuous enough, and surely that was a good angle to bring out in the articles.

"So you'll let me have the records on your local contractors?" Ross's expression was more than ever that of a wolf closing in for a kill.

She braced herself for an explosion from her father. It didn't come.

Instead, he tried to smile. It was a poor facsimile of his usual hearty grin. "I'll have to get permission to release those figures."

He wasn't telling the truth. Her father, the soul of honor, was lying. She sensed it, right down to the marrow of her bones. Her heart clenched, as if something cold and hard tightened around it.

Her father, lying. Ross, hiding something. What was going on?

Please, Lord.

Her thoughts whirled, and then settled on one sure goal. She had to find out what Ross wanted. She had to find out what her father was hiding. And that meant that any hope of keeping her distance from Ross was doomed from the start.

Chapter Four

Ross paced across his office, adrenaline pumping through his system. Lt. Commander Brett Bodine had been hiding something during their interview. He was sure of it. His instincts didn't let him down when it came to detecting evasion.

Too bad those instincts hadn't worked as well in alerting him that his so-called friend had been preparing to stab him in the back to protect the congressman.

He pushed that thought away. He'd been spending too much time brooding about what had happened in Washington. It was fine to use that as motivation—not so good to dwell on his mistakes.

This was a fresh case, and this time he would do all the investigative work himself. He wouldn't give anyone a chance to betray him.

He'd have to be careful with Amanda in that respect. All of her wariness with Ross had returned after that interview with her father. Was it because of Ross's attitude? Or because she, too, had sensed her father's evasiveness?

He didn't know her well enough to be sure what she was thinking, and he probably never would.

Pausing at the window, he looked out at the Cooper River, sunlight sparkling on its surface. A short drive across the new Ravenel Bridge would take him to Patriot's Point and its military displays; a short trip downriver to the harbor brought one to Fort Sumter. Everywhere you looked in the Charleston area you bumped into something related to the military, past or present.

The Bodine family was a big part of that, apparently. Brett Bodine's attitude could simply be the natural caution of a military man when it came to sharing information with the press. Ross didn't believe that, but it was possible.

He'd have to work cautiously, checking and double-checking every fact. Still, he couldn't deny the tingle of excitement that told him he was onto something.

Once he had the list of suppliers that Bodine had so reluctantly agreed to provide, he could start working from that end of the investigation.

Finding the person who was paying the bribes would lead inevitably to the one accepting them.

Sliding into his chair, he pulled out the folder containing the anonymous notes and the transcript of the phone calls. He hadn't felt this energized in over a year. This was the real deal—he could feel it.

He'd just opened the folder when a shadow bisected the band of light from the door he always kept open to the newsroom. He looked up. It was Amanda, with an expression of determination on her face.

"I'd like to speak with you."

Closing the folder, he leveled an I-can't-be-disturbed stare at her. "This isn't a good time."

Instead of backing off, she closed the door behind her and advanced on the desk. "It's important."

"Not now." He ratcheted the stare up to a glare.

Her gaze flickered away from him. Good, intimidation still worked. Amanda believed that her job depended on his goodwill.

Whether it really did, he wasn't so sure. Cyrus seemed to have a soft spot for her, for some reason. But as long as she believed it, she'd do as she was told.

Except that right now, she wasn't. She clasped

her hands together as if she needed support, but she didn't back away.

"What exactly is the slant of the story you're planning to do on the Coast Guard?"

He raised a dismissive brow. "I thought we were clear on this. Your only role is to arrange the interviews, not to contribute to the story, no matter how well you feel you know the subject matter."

"I'm not talking about my contribution. Or lack of it. I want to know what you're after."

"My plans for the story don't concern you."

"They do when you use me to get to my father." She shot the words back at him like arrows.

"Get to him?" Annoyance rose, probably because she was exactly on target. "That implies that he has to be protected from the press."

Those green eyes widened. In shock? Or because she agreed and didn't want him to know it? He expected backpedaling on her part. He didn't get it.

"My father doesn't need protection. But he also doesn't deserve some kind of hatchet job, if that's what you have in mind."

Apparently Amanda could overcome her fear of him when it came to her family.

"Why would you assume that? I'm sure my interview style isn't quite as laid-back as the one you generally employ in your painstaking search for the facts about the latest dog show or charity ball, but that doesn't mean I'm planning a hatchet job."

That was below the belt, and he knew it. After all, he was the one who assigned her those stories. And he'd been the recipient of enough sarcasm from his father to dislike using it on anyone else. Still, he had no choice but to keep Amanda away from the truth.

A faint wash of color came up in her cheeks. "You're after something more than a profile piece, aren't you?"

He stood, forcing her to look up at him. "*You're* an employee of this newspaper, Amanda. If you want to continue in that, I'd suggest you keep your imagination in check. Anything I print about your father or anyone else will be the exact truth."

"I trust it will be." She took a cautious step back. "If it isn't…" She stopped, apparently not able to think of a sufficient threat to end that sentence.

"You don't need to worry about that. I'll make sure of it."

Amanda couldn't know just how much he meant that. He wouldn't make the mistake again of rushing into print without being sure of his ability to back up his facts.

But he also wouldn't give up. He had no desire to hurt Amanda or her family. But if Brett Bodine was involved in a kickback scheme, the world was going to know about it, thanks to him.

She was actually shaking. Amanda detoured to the restroom instead of going straight back to her desk.

One of Cyrus's nicer eccentricities had been to have the women's room copied after the one in an elegant downtown department store, with plush love seats in a small sitting area and art deco black-and-white tile in the restroom. She went straight through, headed for the marble sink with its beveled mirror.

Ridiculous. This was idiotic, to let herself be so affected by what that man said or thought of her. She stared at herself in the mirror, disliking the flushed cheeks. Not only had she been affected, but she'd undoubtedly let him see it.

Grabbing a paper towel, she wet it and pressed it against her cheeks. She couldn't let him get to her like this. This wasn't who she was.

And he hadn't really answered her questions. He hadn't denied or explained anything. He'd stonewalled her, like a crooked politician fending off the press.

She tossed the towel in the trash and touched her hair, smoothing a strand back into place, regaining the polished facade she was careful to present to the world. Well, even if she hadn't gotten the answers she'd gone into Ross's office for, something had been gained. She'd actually confronted Ross Lockhart, and she was still in one piece.

She grimaced at her face in the mirror. More or less, anyway. And she still had her job, although he'd issued a not-so-subtle threat on that score.

Ross had implied that she was imagining the emotional currents that had swirled through the office during that interview. Little though she wanted to believe that, she forced herself to consider the possibility.

She couldn't deny that she tended to rush headlong into her latest crusade. If she did deny it, her loving family would stand in line to protest. There was that incident with the woman who claimed her lawyer had stolen her inheritance. It turned out she had neither lawyer nor inheritance.

Tension had existed between Ross and her father. She certainly hadn't dreamed that up. But it was possible that the two men simply disliked each other. Daddy could well have picked up on her feelings for her annoying new boss over the past few months. She hadn't made a secret of them, certainly.

But that didn't account for her conviction that her father had been hiding something. Brett Bodine never hid anything—everything he thought came right out his mouth. Anyone who knew him knew that. He should have exploded at Ross. He hadn't.

She pushed herself away from the sink. Standing here brooding about it wasn't doing the least bit of good. She had to think this through logically. If she talked to Daddy—

The reluctance she felt to broach the subject shocked her. She'd never hesitated to talk to her father, even though sometimes she'd known she'd have to be prepared to ride out a storm if she did. But then, never before had she suspected that Daddy was lying.

Enough of this. She strode out of the restroom and headed for her desk. She'd forget the whole thing, go and get some supper, maybe call Annabel, just for the assurance of hearing her twin's voice.

But when she rounded the corner of the newsroom, she realized she'd forgotten something. C.J. was there, apparently waiting for her. In Amanda's chair, in fact.

C.J. got up hastily when she spotted Amanda coming. "Hey." She seemed to take a second look at Amanda. "Is somethin' wrong?" Her tone was laced with a kind of reluctant concern.

"No, nothing." She pasted what she hoped was a convincing smile on her face. "I didn't realize you were still here. We don't expect our interns to work late, you know."

C.J.'s face tightened, as if she interpreted that as a criticism. "I was writing up the descriptions of the Coast Guard base, like you asked me to. Or was that just busywork to keep me out of the way?"

Amanda pressed her lips together. The truth was that she'd forgotten all about giving C.J. that assignment, and the kid was astute enough to know that. She cleared her mind and prepared to deal with the problem in front of her.

"The assignment isn't busywork, but it's true that I need to get a sense of where your writing is now. And it wouldn't have been appropriate to take an intern to that sort of interview. You see that, don't you?"

C.J. nodded, perhaps a bit reluctantly.

"Okay, then. Let's have a look at what you've written."

The intern put a couple of sheets of paper in front of her on the desk. "I was just doing some rewriting on the printouts. If you want, I can input the changes and print it out again."

So C.J. wanted to present her with the best work possible. That was a good sign.

"Not necessary. Believe me, I've deciphered worse than this."

She breathed a silent prayer as she bent over the sheets, hoping she wouldn't have to correct too much. Cyrus had handpicked his intern, and Cyrus was erratic enough to make the decision based on whatever standard he thought important at the moment.

But C.J.'s writing proved to be surprisingly smooth and insightful. She read it once, quickly, and then went back over it again, checking a few places. Finally she looked up at the young woman, recognizing the tension that emanated from C.J.

"Relax, C.J. This is good, very good."

C.J.'s breath came out in a whoosh of relief. "Thanks." She seemed to make an effort to sound blasé, but a hint of eagerness showed through. "You marked some things, though."

"Let's take a look." At her gesture, C.J. pulled up her chair. She held the papers flat so that they could go over them together.

"This is a very effective word picture." She tapped one paragraph. "Notice how you've used exact details to get the image across. Now, down here, the observation isn't quite as visual. Do you see what I mean?"

"Got it." C.J. scribbled a few words on the sheet, seeming determined to get it exactly right. She flipped to the second page. "It's the same thing here, isn't it?" She stabbed another paragraph with her pen.

"You've got it."

C.J. slashed an arrow and then began making notes on the back of the sheet.

"You can go home," Amanda said gently. "You don't have to work on it right now."

C.J. moved her shoulders restlessly. "It's hard to get anything done there. The landlord turned off the air-conditioning. He says it's broke, but everyone thinks he's just trying to save money."

"In this heat? How long has it been off?"

"Ten days, maybe. My grandmother's been takin' a walk to the market every day, just so she can go in where it's cool."

That was unconscionable, as hot as the weather had been. Her mind flickered to the cool, welcoming dimness of her small carriage house apartment.

"Hasn't anyone complained to the landlord?"

"Doesn't do any good. He's always cutting corners like that—keeping it hot in summer and cold in winter. Besides, folks figure if they complain too much, he'll treat them even worse."

"But—"

C.J. shook her head. "No use talking about it. I'd rather work."

A relatively polite way of telling Amanda it was none of her business. She watched as the intern went over her work again, scribbling eagerly.

Had she had that sort of initiative at C.J.'s age? She doubted it. She'd been excited to get off to college, true, but she'd been looking forward to starting over with new people, creating a different identity for herself other than just being one of the Bodines. She'd been as excited about football games and parties as about what she might learn.

C.J. looked up from the page. "If I do this whole thing again, will you read it and tell me what you think?"

"Sure thing." She smiled, pleased at the sign C.J. was willing to accept criticism and learn from it. "You have a lot of drive, don't you?"

C.J. shrugged, but this time there wasn't any sullenness attached. "My grandmother always tells me that if I want something, it's my job to do what it takes to get it."

Her thoughts flickered to Miz Callie. "You

know, my grandmother would say exactly the same thing. I guess we have that in common."

Amanda half expected C.J. to back away from that suggestion. Instead, she got a tentative smile that revealed an eager, slightly scared young woman behind the tough exterior.

Another piece of Miz Callie's advice popped into her mind. *God sends people into our lives for a reason, Amanda. Always watch for that, because He might have a special job for you to do.*

Maybe C.J. was destined to be one of those people for her.

Ross locked his office door and started down the hallway, his steps echoing emptily on the tile. He'd stayed at the computer long after the editorial offices had grown quiet, familiarizing himself with every tidbit of information that might possibly affect the investigation.

Speaking of tidbits, his stomach had finally convinced him it was time to quit. Lunch was a distant memory, and he wouldn't achieve anything useful by checking out the snack machine.

He paused automatically at the newsroom door. His attention sharpened. Someone was still there. In a few quiet steps, he had a clear view.

Amanda sat at her desk, her attention riveted

on the computer screen. A strand of that sleek brown hair swung forward, brushing her cheek, and the glasses she habitually wore for computer work had slid down her nose, giving her a slightly disheveled look. Charming, but not her usual polished veneer.

Staying late to work didn't fit with the image he had of her as the belle of the social ball. But then, he'd already figured out that there was more to Amanda Bodine than his snap judgment of her.

She'd found the courage to stand up to him today. While he didn't welcome opposition, especially from a subordinate, he had to admire the grit it had taken.

He'd come down too hard on her, that was the truth, and it had been nagging at him for a couple of hours now. That conscience his grandmother had instilled in him could be a troublesome thing at times.

He didn't want to feel that he'd been unfair to her. But he couldn't ignore the truth.

Besides, he still needed her. Threatening to fire her wouldn't encourage her father to come across with any information.

He realized he was gritting his teeth, and he forced his jaw to relax. Mending fences was clearly indicated. He'd never been especially good at that.

He walked toward Amanda's desk. At the sound of footsteps she looked up, startled. When she recognized him, she slicked her hair back behind her ear with one finger and slipped the glasses off her face. He couldn't mistake the aura of defensiveness that wrapped around her.

"Amanda." He lifted an eyebrow, trying not to look intimidating. "What keeps you at the office so late?"

Her eyes widened, as if his genial tone was cause for astonishment. "I…I came back after supper to do a little work."

He leaned against the corner of her desk, moving a silver-framed photo so that he wouldn't knock it over, looking at it as he did so. Amanda and her twin, her parents, the two older brothers, all in jackets and jeans and looking windblown as they walked on the beach. A nice family portrait. His gut tightened.

"Doing some research for a story?"

"Not exactly." Her lips pursed, as if trying to decide how much to tell him. The sight distracted him for a moment.

He managed a smile. "It doesn't matter to the boss if you're doing some early Christmas shopping online."

That surprised her into a smile, and some of the

wariness evaporated from her face. "It's nothing like that. I'm looking into some family history for my grandmother, and I can get better access to records through the newspaper."

"Family history?" He perched on the edge of the desk. It was proving easier than he'd expected to get past the barriers he'd erected between them this afternoon. "I should have thought your grandmother was an expert on that."

"She is the family historian, but..." She paused, fiddling with the silver chain that hung around her neck. He had a sense that she was weighing what and how much to tell him.

"But what?"

"It's sort of a...a bit of a family mystery."

The stammer was a dead giveaway that poised, in-control Amanda didn't want to tell him about it, whatever it was. That just increased his curiosity.

"A mystery?" he said lightly. "Sounds intriguing. Tell me about it."

"Well, I..." She bit her lip. "It has to do with a distant relative who dropped from sight during World War II. My grandmother is determined to find out what happened to him, and I promised to help her."

It didn't escape his attention that she was

carefully editing what she said to him. Well, fair enough.

If he could gain her trust by helping her with her little genealogical problem, it might ease things between them in other ways.

"This relative—was he in the service?"

She nodded. "He ran away from home to enlist, as far as we can tell."

"That's simple, then. The military records—"

She was shaking her head, and that recalcitrant strand of hair swung back against her cheek again. His hand itched to smooth it back for her, and he clamped down on the ridiculous urge.

"It's not that easy. He apparently signed up under a false name. That's what upsets my grandmother—the possibility of never knowing what happened to him."

He didn't know a lot about World War II, but the problem intrigued him. "You're assuming he died in service, are you?"

"I guess we are. I'd think he'd have gotten in touch with the family sometime if he'd come back safely."

He prodded the problem with his mind, intrigued in spite of himself. How would you go about tracing someone in those circumstances?

"That is tricky. Would he have enlisted locally?" He shook his head. "Probably not, if he didn't want to be recognized. Unless he wasn't very well-known."

"That's a thought." She absently slid the hair back behind her ear, frowning at the screen. "I was trying to look at enlistments from Charleston, but you're right. He'd have been recognized for sure if he'd gone there. But if he went someplace else, how do I begin finding him?"

He pulled over the office chair from the adjoining desk and sat down next to her. He didn't miss the involuntary darkening of her eyes at his closeness. Didn't miss it, but tried to ignore it, just as he tried to ignore his own longing to put his hand on her arm.

"Do you know anything about the circumstances? Exactly when he enlisted? Did he have a car? Any other means of traveling very far? Where were the enlistment centers in the area?"

"Some of that I know." A smile tugged at the corners of her mouth. "But you're pretty good at this investigative stuff, aren't you?"

"I should be. It comes with the job. Any journalist should have an overdeveloped sense of curiosity."

Her eyebrows lifted. "I have to admit I'm wondering why you're so eager to help me with this. This afternoon…"

"Maybe that's why." He forced the words out, not used to apologizing. "I guess I owe you an apology. I came on pretty strong."

Her eyebrows lifted. "Are you sure you want to admit that?"

"All the books on managing staff say that the good boss admits when he's wrong."

"I see." The dimple next to the corner of her lips showed briefly. "I'm delighted to know that you're trying to be a good boss. Is scaring everyone in the building half to death part of that?"

Was he really enjoying this semiflirtatious exchange? Maybe he ought to back away, but he discovered that he didn't want to.

"You're exaggerating. Nobody is that intimidated by me."

Her eyes widened in mock surprise. "Then why does Billy run in the other direction every time he sees you?"

"Billy?" He tried to think of a newsroom staffer by that name and failed. "Who's Billy?"

"Billy Bradley. The mail room boy who delivers mail to your office several times a day." Her expression said that he should have known that. "I'm sure those books of yours would tell you that a good boss knows something about all of his people."

"Maybe so." He could pull back from the intimacy of this conversation at any moment. Maybe he should. But he didn't want to. "If you're so smart, tell me three things about Billy Bradley."

"That's easy. Billy helps his mother support two younger brothers. He plays soccer in the little spare time he has. And he longs to be an investigative reporter."

"Wants to break big stories, does he?" He knew that feeling. "He won't do that from the mail room."

"He has those two little brothers and the widowed mother, remember?" Her tone chided him gently. "At this point, he's happy just to be working for a newspaper while he dreams of big stories. He's determined to be the best mail room boy ever."

"I see he has a big cheerleader in you." He could almost empathize with the kid. Still, he'd never had to work his way up through the mail room. A position had opened up automatically for the congressman's son.

"I like to encourage people." The dimple peeked out again.

Intrigued by the dimple, he leaned toward her,

his gaze on her face. He saw her eyes widen and her pupils darken as he neared. A pulse beat visibly in her neck, and he fought the urge to touch it, even to put his lips over hers.

Whoa. Back off. He couldn't do that. He was her boss. They were in the newsroom. Was he asking to be charged with harassment?

He eased away from her, seeing the recognition in her eyes that must mirror his. They were attracted. Okay, they both got it. And they also both got that they couldn't act on that attraction.

He got up, the chair rolling soundlessly back. "Well. I'd better get on my way. Let me know if any of my suggestions pay off."

"Suggestions?" For an instant her eyes were glazed. Then she blinked and glanced toward the computer screen. "Yes, right. Thank you." She took an audible breath. "Good night, Ross."

"Good night." He turned and walked quickly away before he could give in to any of the impulses that rocketed through him.

Chapter Five

Amanda's steps hastened as she went up the stairs to the beach house. It had been a tense day in many ways, mostly because of Ross, and she was relieved to be on the island, safe from the pressures of the newsroom.

She wasn't sure what she'd expected after those moments she and Ross had alone in the newsroom last night. Maybe a little easing of his attitude toward her, at least, or a sense that he remembered.

Instead he'd been curt to the point of rudeness all day. She'd finally escaped the newsroom, taking C.J. with her. They'd wandered around the Market—Charleston's venerable open-air institution. She'd been gathering photos and interviews over the summer with some of the women who made sweetgrass baskets, hoping at some point she'd be able to do a story on them. Certainly it was more interesting than most of the pieces she did.

She hurried inside. "Miz Callie?"

"Right here, darlin'." Her grandmother emerged from the kitchen, beaming at the sight of her, and enveloped her in a hug. "Did you remember the rolls?"

"I sure did." She handed over the bag of still-warm rolls from the Magnolia Bakery and brushed a kiss on Miz Callie's soft cheek.

Sometimes she thought that no one in her life ever expressed such obvious pleasure at the sight of her. It was a good feeling, to be so clearly loved, and every one of Miz Callie's grandchildren knew it.

"Supper's almost ready, and Georgia and Matt and little Lindsay are joining us. Come along in."

They found Georgia in the kitchen, forking fried chicken onto an ironstone platter. Through the glass doors, Amanda could see her cousin's fiancé, Matt Harper, and his eight-year-old daughter, Lindsay, knocking the sand off their shoes. They must have walked across the beach from Matt's house next door.

She went to open the sliding door for them and stood for a moment, inhaling the wind-borne salt scent of the sea. The tide was out, leaving long tidal pools and a swath of wet sand that glistened, beckoning her to plant some footprints there among the ghost crab trails.

"Hi, Amanda." Matt, tall and tanned, bent to press his cheek briefly against hers. "It's good to see you. Lindsay, come give Amanda a hug, honey."

Matt was beginning to sound like a good old boy after nearly a year on the South Carolina coast. As for Lindsay, she looked like all of them had when they were children, sun kissed and wind tousled.

"Hey, sugar, how are you?" Amanda gave the child a quick hug. "I declare, you've grown an inch this summer."

Lindsay grinned, displaying a space where a front tooth used to be. "Maybe I'll be the tallest one in my class when school starts."

"Could be." If she'd inherited Matt's height, she might well be.

Lindsay crossed the kitchen immediately to wrap her arms around Georgia's waist. Georgia said that she and Matt were taking their relationship slowly because of the child, but it looked to her as if Lindsay was ready to claim Georgia as her mother.

"Everyone grab a dish to take to the table," Miz Callie declared. "It's ready."

Amanda watched her cousin during the cheerful bustle of getting the food on. Georgia had never looked happier. The glow in her face when she looked at Matt and Lindsay shouted her love to the world.

Amanda suppressed a tiny pang that might have been jealousy. Georgia deserved every bit of the happiness she was experiencing. It was childish to use that as a reason to wonder when or if it might happen for her.

Once the blessing had been said and the platters of food started around the table, Georgia fixed her with an enquiring glance. "What's wrong, Manda? You look like someone's been picking on you. Is it that boss of yours again?"

"Not exactly." She forked a golden chicken breast onto her plate. "He's…" Her wayward imagination took her back to those moments when she'd felt lost in Ross's warm gaze. "Sometimes he can be human. He actually gave me a few pointers on the search for Ned."

Georgia dropped the spoon she held into the mashed potatoes. "You didn't tell that newspaper editor about Ned. For goodness' sake, Amanda…"

"Relax, honey. I didn't tell him anything

except that I was trying to find out what happened to a relative of my grandmother's. He's an outsider. He's not going to know that old story."

"You said he helped you?" Miz Callie leaned forward, blue eyes bright with the question. "Did you find something?"

"Not exactly, but he gave me some ideas. For instance, Ned wouldn't have enlisted in Charleston, because he'd have been recognized there. And if he didn't have access to a car—"

"He didn't," Miz Callie said surely. "Goodness, it was so tough to drive then, with gas rationing and all, that folks just didn't drive anyplace they could get to by some other means."

"That's what I thought, so I've started checking up on buses and trains. Seems like he'd go someplace within fairly easy reach."

"I suppose he could have gotten someone to drive him," Miz Callie cautioned. "Though if so, he still couldn't have gone far, what with the rationing."

"Is there a record of where all the enlistment offices were in '42?" Matt asked.

"There must be. I'm working on that. And on what name he might have used."

"Eat, sugar," her grandmother said. "You don't need to let your supper get cold while you tell us."

Amanda put a forkful of fragrant fried chicken into her mouth, relishing the flavor. Maybe Miz Callie's fried chicken wasn't good for you, as her mother reminded the family each time she tried yet another vegetarian entrée, but it surely was delicious.

"What name would he have used?" Matt asked. "A middle name? A family name?"

"That's a thought. We ought to make up a list of possibilities to check out." Georgia traced her fork along the tablecloth, as if writing a list. "I'm getting excited all over again, just talking about it. I think Manda's really onto something."

She could search through military records, using some of the family names this time. For an instant she was back in front of her computer, with Ross so close she could smell the fresh scent of his aftershave.

She didn't want to keep remembering that, but she couldn't seem to stop herself.

She'd have to find a way. Ross's curtness today had to mean that he regretted what happened. Recognized it and regretted it.

That was the best course, surely. Nothing real could ever develop between them, and she'd be smart to accept that.

She forced her attention back to the table.

Matt had begun telling an anecdote about one of his clients, an elderly man who wanted to sue his landlord for letting pigeons roost on the gables of the house he rented over in Mount Pleasant's old town.

She laughed with the rest of them, but the story reminded her of C.J.'s housing problems. Matt, as an attorney, might have some insight.

"What if you had a tenant with a real problem? For instance, he or she had a landlord who refused to fix the air-conditioning in a building where folks were really suffering from the heat."

"I'd have to know a bit more about it to give advice." Matt focused on her. "But certainly they have legal recourse if they have a signed lease that includes air-conditioning. It's a violation of the warrant of habitability. Is this someone you know?"

"In a way. My intern at work. She lives with her grandmother somewhere in Charleston, and they're having a lot of trouble with the landlord."

Matt frowned. "Too often, people are afraid to fight in situations like that. Or they can't afford to." His lips twitched as Georgia and Amanda both looked at him. "And, yes, I would take a case like that pro bono, if that's what you're planning to ask me. But as I said, I'd need a lot more information."

"I can talk to C.J., my intern, about it." Amanda recognized the enthusiasm that gripped her. It was what her brothers liked to call her Joan of Arc response to the little guy getting hurt.

Well, good. Maybe it would keep her distracted from the stupid attraction she kept feeling for Ross.

"Well, now, Amanda, it seems this might be just what you've been looking for."

Amanda stared blankly at her grandmother. Had Miz Callie been reading her mind?

"You've been talking about wanting to write an important story, haven't you?" Miz Callie said. "Seems to me you've just found one."

The idea took root with a sureness that made it seem as if God was sending a message to her through Miz Callie. She reached over to squeeze her grandmother's hand.

"You know, you might be right about that."

If this guy got any more evasive, Ross decided, he just might slide right out of the booth at the coffee shop and on out the door.

"Your contracts with the Coast Guard base must be pretty important to your business, Mr. Gerard," he prompted.

The list of suppliers had finally come through from Amanda's father, and he'd picked Gerard

Plumbing as a good place to start. Now he was starting to wonder about that. Amos Gerard had balked at coming to the newspaper, but finally agreed to meet for a cup of coffee at the coffee shop across the street. So far the coffee was the only thing that had crossed his lips.

Gerard shrugged, wiping a ham-size palm on his jeans. "I guess so. They're good folks to work with." His gaze shifted from the coffee cup to the spoon to the sugar bowl without coming to rest on Ross.

"How did you come by that contract?"

He considered himself pretty good at reading the people he interviewed, but he couldn't decide whether the man had something to hide or was just nervous at talking to someone from the press.

"Saw the announcement and bid on it, like everyone else." Now Gerard's gaze did meet his, but with a suspicious glare. "If you're saying there was anything wrong with my work, you're way off base. The Coast Guard got exactly what they ordered from me, and at a fair price, too."

"I'm not questioning your work at all," he said quickly. If Gerard thought that, he'd clam up entirely. "I'd just like some insight into how the contracts are awarded. Who decides on the supplier, and how they make that decision."

Gerard's cheeks rounded, and he puffed out a breath. "I guess they decide who can do the job cheapest, same as everyone else does."

"It's a valuable contract for the supplier. Maybe there's a little extra consideration expected if your company is chosen."

He'd expect an honest man to take offense at the comment. Gerard just stared at him blankly. Then his gaze slid away again. "I guess…"

He let that trail off, his eyes riveted on the person who had just come into the coffee shop and was coming straight toward them. Amanda Bodine.

Something that might have been anger washed over Gerard's face and was gone so quickly Ross couldn't be sure of what he'd seen. Then he slid from the booth, tossing a handful of change on the table.

"We're done," he said, and walked quickly away with a curt nod to Amanda as he passed her.

Ross stared after him, speculation flooding his mind. Had Gerard been about to admit something? And if he had, was it the sight of one of the Bodines that had changed his mind? He didn't want to read too much into that, but Amanda's entrance had done something.

She paused at his table. "I'm glad I caught you. There's something I'd like to—"

He cut her off with a jerk of his head in the direction of the closing door. "Do you know the man who just left?"

She turned to look out the plate-glass window at the retreating figure. Gerard's Plumbing was clearly visible on the back of his shirt. Her brow furrowed.

"Gerard's Plumbing? I think they've done some work for my folks over the years. I don't think I know him personally. Is there some work you need done?"

That encounter could mean something or nothing, but all his instincts told him that Gerard had been a little too eager to get away from him once he'd spotted Amanda Bodine.

In any event, he couldn't afford to let Amanda start inquiring into what he was doing.

"Just a casual conversation." He rose, putting his payment on top of the bill. "I'm headed back to the office. I'll let you get your coffee."

Instead of heading for the counter, she fell into step beside him. "I really wanted to talk with you. About a story idea."

"Bring it up at the editorial meeting."

She stayed doggedly at his side, and her face was alive with enthusiasm. "C.J. told me about something that's going on in the apartment block where she and her grandmother live. It seems the landlord is refusing to take care of routine maintenance, not even getting the air-conditioning fixed in this heat."

They stepped out onto the sidewalk as she spoke, and the hot, humid air settled on him like a wet wool blanket. Trying to ignore it—ignore her—he strode across the street.

"That's not a story, Amanda. It's a personal annoyance. C.J. and her grandmother should complain."

"To whom?" She had to hurry to keep up with him. "The landlord ignores the tenants, and from what I can tell, they're too afraid of being kicked out to raise a fuss. He shouldn't be allowed to get away with that. If we ran a story—"

He stopped in front of the building, then immediately wished he'd taken the conversation on inside to the lobby. Where it was cool.

He scowled at her. That didn't seem to dampen the zeal that shone in her green eyes. "I repeat, it's not a story. The landlord could have a dozen perfectly good explanations, and you don't know any of them."

"But—"

"You're a reporter, Amanda, not a social worker or a crusader."

She flushed a little at that. "If I got more information about the landlord, talked to the tenants, then would you consider running it?"

That was the last thing he needed, to have Amanda running off half-cocked and getting herself into trouble. He was starting to feel responsible for her, and that annoyed him.

"Just let it go, Amanda. Get on with the article you already have on tap. If there's anything in this—"

"There is," she interrupted, anger sparking in her eyes.

"That decision is mine to make, not yours."

He held the door open, welcoming the blast of cool air. He could have someone look into the situation and get a handle on whether this was worth an investigation, but that someone wasn't going to be Amanda. If by any chance that landlord was pulling something underhanded and probably illegal on his tenants, he wouldn't be too happy to be confronted by a reporter.

For a moment Amanda stood on the hot sidewalk, glaring at him. Then, chin held high, she marched into the building.

He followed, letting the door swing shut behind him. Amanda was already almost to the elevator. Maybe he'd use the stairs.

She'd taken offense at his decision, not surprisingly. What else was new? It seemed impossible for the two of them to meet on neutral ground. He constantly fought the urge to throttle her.

Or kiss her.

Chapter Six

"Come on, can't you give me a smile?" Amanda coaxed, watching the child's face in the screen of her digital camera. "Please?"

The little girl sat at the top of the sliding board, dark hair in multiple braids tied with pink ribbons that matched the pink shorts and T-shirt she wore, her lips pressed together firmly.

Amanda glanced at C.J., who'd accompanied her on this assignment. "She'd be an adorable example of the summer playground program if we could get a smile."

C.J. took the hint and crawled onto the bottom of the slide. "Hey, is this the right way to use this thing?" She planted her palms on the slide and made as if to pull herself up toward the girl. "Is it?"

The child shook her head, solemn for another

moment. "No." The corners of her lips curved up just a bit.

"It must be." C.J. pretended to scramble upward. "How'd you get up there? You slid up on your tummy, didn't you?"

"No, ma'am!" The child grinned, eyes lighting up. She grabbed the sides of the slide. "You get yourself outta the way, y'hear? 'Cause I'm comin' down."

Amanda snapped quickly while C.J. scrambled out of the way. The child sailed off the end, bounced on her feet, and was headed toward the ladder again when a whistle blew.

"Crafts!" she yelled, and darted off toward the pavilion.

A smile lingering on her lips, Amanda shaded the camera with her hand to check the photos she'd taken, aware of C.J. watching over her shoulder. To Amanda's amusement, C.J. now wore a neat pair of tan slacks with a shirt in Amanda's favorite shade of turquoise.

The intern's attitude had steadily improved since that pugnacious exchange the first day, which was certainly an answer to prayer. Maybe the plain talking Amanda had done had gotten through to her.

Amanda knew perfectly well that she was

putting off another serious discussion. She'd spent a couple of hours with C.J. today, and she hadn't mentioned the housing issue or the possibility of doing a story on it.

Maybe because that wasn't really a possibility, not as far as Ross was concerned. Amanda's jaw tightened at the thought. He was being unreasonable, dismissing the idea just because it came from her.

"Why didn't they send a photographer with us?" C.J.'s question was abrupt, as if she was ready to take offense at their lack of a photographer. "I thought they had pros to do the pictures."

"The paper does have a few photographers, but not enough to go around." And too often, the stories she was assigned weren't considered important enough to warrant a photographer. "If you have a chance to learn anything about digital photography, grab it. That ability improves your chances in a tough job market, believe me."

C.J. frowned a little, but she nodded. "Did we get enough material from Miz Dottie for the story, do you think?"

Amanda glanced across the playground to the pavilion. A couple of eager high school volunteers were teaching crafts under the benign gaze of the elderly black woman who'd spearheaded the fight to provide this program for the poorest of the city's children.

"I hope so. There's plenty more I'd like to say about Miz Dottie, but we're going to have limited column inches for this story."

That fact annoyed her. In her opinion, Miz Dottie was a true hero—a woman who'd dedicated her life to her community, sturdily walking over the forces that would have stopped her.

But the paper, in the person of Ross, wouldn't spare precious space for what he'd dismiss as a "feel-good" story. The old newspaper adage that "if it bleeds, it leads," seemed to be his motto.

She lifted damp hair off her neck. The stifling heat didn't seem to bother the kids, but she was wilting. "Let's head back to the office and pull this together."

They walked across the playground together, Amanda mentally composing the lead to the story.

"So if I learn to use a camera, I should put that on a résumé." C.J.'s mind was obviously on her future, not the current story, but Amanda didn't blame her for that. This internship ought to prepare her for a career.

"Definitely," Amanda said. She hesitated, knowing the intern was prickly on the subject of higher education for herself. "You know, there are still plenty of loans and scholarships—"

"Not for me," C.J. cut her off. "You don't get it. I have my grandmother to take care of. She took me in after my mamma died. Now it's my turn."

"I understand. Really." Wouldn't she do the same for Miz Callie, if she were in C.J.'s situation?

They got into the car, and she turned the air to high, the movement reminding her again of C.J.'s problem with her landlord. But this time Miz Callie's opinions on that subject came to the forefront of her mind.

Miz Callie thought she was meant to tackle this issue. If so, she'd have to risk disobeying Ross's orders. And now was the time.

Come on, Amanda. Are you a woman or a mouse?

She glanced in the rearview mirror and pulled out into traffic. "Is the situation with your hot apartment any better?"

C.J. concentrated on fastening her seat belt. "Not much. I bought a fan. Gran sits in front of it and works on her baskets."

"Baskets?"

"She makes sweetgrass baskets for the Market."

"I didn't know that. I wonder if I've talked to her there. I've been collecting interviews and photos to do a piece on the sweetgrass basket weavers."

C.J. glanced at her, lifting her brows. "D'you actually think he'll let you run it?"

There was no doubt in Amanda's mind as to who that "he" was. She probably shouldn't encourage C.J.'s attitude toward Ross, but she had to be honest in her answer.

"I don't know. But I want to try. Preserving that heritage seems important to me." The Gullah people of the islands had brought their basket-weaving skills with them from Africa generations ago. Without the dedication of the few who remained, the art would be lost, just another beautiful thing swept away by changing times. "Would your grandmother talk to me about the craft?"

"I guess. Long as you're not going to make her look like an ignorant old woman."

She gave C.J. a level look. "Do you think I'd do that?"

C.J. returned the look, seeming to measure her. "No," she said finally.

The level of trust contained in the word pleased her, but now she had to ask the more challenging question.

Please help me, Lord, to do the right thing for the right reason. That was the tricky part, wasn't it? Miz Callie would say that the Lord expected not only the right actions, but the right heart.

"I was thinking about what you told me about your landlord. Would your grandmother and some of the other tenants talk to me about it? Maybe—"

"You can't put them in the paper." C.J.'s voice rose. "He'd kick us out for sure."

"But maybe just the threat of publicity would be enough to make him mend his ways." Amanda hoped she was right about that. "I have a friend who's an attorney. He's willing to make sure your rights are protected."

"We can't afford a lawyer." C.J.'s face closed, turning her back into the sullen teenager she'd seemed in their first encounter.

"It wouldn't cost you anything. He's a friend of mine." She smiled. "And you're a friend."

C.J. averted her face, staring out the window at the busy sidewalks, crowded with locals headed for their favorite lunchtime restaurants and tourists bedecked with cameras. The intern was silent for so long that Amanda was sure she'd blown it.

C.J. traced a line down the crease of her slacks with one finger. "I guess maybe we could talk about it, anyway. See what my gran says."

Amanda let out a breath she hadn't known she was holding. "I can't ask for more than that. I'll stop by this evening, okay?"

C.J.'s gaze, dark with what seemed a lifetime of doubt, met hers. "Okay."

Surely, if the door was opening to this, God meant her to walk through.

"This isn't one of your brightest ideas, Manda." Hugh, Amanda's next older brother, peered disapprovingly at the apartment building where C.J. lived that evening. "Reminds me of the time you rushed into the neighbor's house, convinced it was on fire because you saw an orange glow in the bedroom window, which turned out to be mood lighting."

Would no one ever let her forget that? "This is different."

"Let me go in with you, okay?"

"No way. C.J.'s leery enough of talking to me. Confronted with you, she'd clam up entirely."

"Why?" He tried to make all six foot four of himself look innocuous. He didn't succeed. "I'm harmless."

"You know that and I know that, but oddly enough, most people find you intimidating. Useful in law enforcement, but not in this." She patted his tanned cheek. "Thanks for driving me. I sure wouldn't want to leave my car on the street in this block."

"Then you ought to understand why I don't want to leave my sister in this block," he retorted, fixing her with the look that probably made wrongdoers confess on the spot.

"Just be a good brother and come back for me in about an hour and a half. If I'm going to be longer, I'll call you."

Hugh, probably knowing from a lifetime of experience that he couldn't dissuade her, nodded. "Daddy would scalp me if he knew I let you come here after dark. And you, too."

True, this wasn't an area she'd normally frequent, but she hadn't been able to come until C.J. got home from her job waiting tables. At this hour, the stoops and sidewalks were empty of children playing and women gossiping. A couple of men came out of the tavern across the street, talking loudly, and a group of teenage males drifted down the street, silent as smoke.

"I'll be fine." She slid out before she could change her mind. "See you later."

Despite her bravado, she was relieved that he waited at the curb, his size intimidating, until she'd been buzzed into the building. Once the door shut behind her, she waved through the glass. Hugh got back into his car and drove off.

There were definite advantages to having big brothers, annoying as they could be sometimes. She checked the row of mailboxes to be sure she had the number right and headed for the stairs.

She picked her way up, avoiding a few broken risers, her forehead damp with sweat before she reached the landing. The air was stifling, and the handrail had come away from the wall, dangling uselessly. That couldn't make it easy for C.J.'s grandmother to get up and down. Whether the landlord had done anything illegal she didn't know, but he certainly wasn't taking care of his building.

The apartment C.J. shared with her grandmother was on the third floor. She arrived slightly out of breath and knocked. C.J. opened the door almost before she'd taken her hand down.

"Hi, C.J." She hoped she sounded as if this visit was a normal thing for them. "I hope I'm not late."

C.J. shook her head, glancing back over her shoulder into the apartment. "My gran's not... Well, she's not real happy about this. She doesn't feel so good tonight."

"No wonder, hot as it is." She looked pointedly beyond the intern.

C.J. opened the door wider and motioned her

in. "You're welcome to come in. I'm just letting you know how things stand."

Amanda stepped into a living room that was hot and airless, but scrupulously clean. Handmade lace doilies topped the backs of chairs and set under lamps. But it wasn't the doilies that captured Amanda's interest. It was the baskets.

Sweetgrass baskets, handmade by a master weaver, sat on every surface. A large one held newspapers and magazines, while a half dozen smaller ones were in use for everything from fruit to balls of yarn.

She picked up a shallow serving basket, its top edge intricately braided, the base striped in tan and brown that reminded her of the marshes in winter. "This is beautiful."

"You know what that basket is for?" A sharp voice cracked the question.

Amanda turned, basket balanced on her palms, to see the erect elderly woman who stood in the doorway of what must be a bedroom. She was tiny, but she held herself erect with the dignity of a judge. Maybe she was a judge, at that, because she studied Amanda as if weighing her heart.

"Yes, ma'am. It's a pie basket, isn't it? My grandmother has one like it."

The woman inclined her head in a slight nod,

as if awarding Amanda a point. "I heah from my granddaughter that you're a Bodine. Miz Callie your grandma?"

"She is."

Another point. She set down the basket. Judging by the perspiration that glistened on the elderly woman's skin, they ought to sit down and take advantage of the breeze from the fan C.J. must have put in the front window. But she could hardly suggest it. Apparently, the woman hadn't made up her mind whether Amanda was welcome or not.

"Gran, this is Amanda Bodine." C.J. rushed the introduction, sounding rattled. Well, she was standing between two of the authority figures in her life. "Amanda, I'd like to introduce my grandmother, Miz Etta Carrey."

"Miz Carrey, I'm glad to meet you. We think a lot of C.J. at the newspaper."

That must have been the wrong thing to say, because the woman's lips tightened. "My grandchild says you're talking about putting something in the paper about our troubles with the landlord. She shouldn't have mentioned our business. It's private."

Nothing like getting right to the heart of the matter. "If your landlord is breaking the terms of your lease, it's not right. Maybe the threat of publicity will do what complaints won't."

"Maybe it would, maybe it wouldn't. We're not going to know, 'cause you're not writing anything about us for that newspaper."

"Gran—"

"You, hush." The woman turned on C.J., dark eyes snapping. "You think he's not gonna know it came from us if something's in that paper, with you working there every day? Next thing we'll be out in the street, lucky if we get our belongings out with us."

"Amanda has a lawyer she says would help us."

"No!" The woman showed the first sign of strain, reaching out to grasp the door frame, her hand twisted by arthritis. "It can't be, Catherine Jane, and you should know that. You can't go against your family, just because of that job at the newspaper."

For an instant Amanda didn't know who she meant, but of course C.J. must stand for Catherine Jane. An elegant name, but one that must sound hopelessly old-fashioned to a teenager.

C.J. went quickly to put her arm around the elderly woman's waist. "I'm not, Gran. I'm not." She sent Amanda a look that seemed to say this was her fault. Which, she guessed, it was. "You'd better go."

Miz Callie would say that a lady always knew when to end a call. That apparently was now.

Amanda nodded and moved to the door. "I'm glad to have met you, Miz Carrey. I hope sometime you'll let me talk to you about your baskets."

C.J. pulled the door open, all but shoving Amanda through. "Just go," she muttered. She closed the door firmly in her face.

Amanda started back down the stairs, her stomach twisting. That had been short, but not sweet. She hadn't handled it well. She ought to have… Well, she didn't know what. She felt as if she'd stumbled in the dark and didn't know where she was.

She'd thought she was doing the right thing. Maybe the truth was that she was doing what she so often did—rush into a situation on impulse instead of waiting for guidance. Just as Hugh had pointed out.

She'd reached the sidewalk, with the building door closed behind her, before she recognized an unpalatable fact. She was in trouble. Hugh wasn't coming for her for over an hour, and this wasn't a place to stand around with a handbag and a camera slung over her shoulder. At night. Alone.

A burst of noise and music spilled out of the bar across the street. She took a couple of hurried steps toward the curb. The bar wasn't the sort of place she'd normally enter, but at least there'd be people around while she waited for Hugh. She dragged her cell phone out to call him, its screen a welcome light in the dark.

She'd reached the curb when she saw them— figures, hardly recognizable in the dim light. The teenage boys she'd noticed going in? Maybe. They drifted closer, and her stomach turned over.

Hugh really would have something to say about this. She should have called him before she ever left the building. She glanced behind her. If she ran for the door, could she get inside before one of them reached her? With a shiver that must have been fear, she knew the answer was no.

Fragments of advice from the self-defense class she and Annabel had taken jostled in her mind. Fight? Run?

Before she could decide, a car sped down the street and screeched to a stop next to her. The driver leaned across to open the door.

"Get in. Now." Ross sounded fully as angry as she'd been imagining her brother to be. Maybe more so.

Never mind. She was too glad to see him. She slid into the car and slammed the door.

Chapter Seven

Ross wasn't sure which emotion was stronger—
sheer anger that Amanda had put herself in
danger by disobeying a direct order or the fierce
protectiveness that had swept him when he'd
seen her on that curb. Now that he knew she was
safe, it was probably anger.

"What were you thinking?" he erupted, accel-
erating down the dark street. "Did I or did I not
tell you to leave that story alone? Instead of listening, you walk right into a situation a ten-year-
old child would know better than to get into."

Speaking of listening, she didn't appear to be
paying the least attention to his tirade. Instead,
she was twisted around in the seat, staring out the
back at something behind them.

"What are you doing? Is someone following us?"

"No." She turned around again.

In the light of an overhanging streetlamp, he caught a quick, clear image of her face before shadows fell over it again. Her expression stifled any words that were on his lips.

Fear. Amanda—behind that cool, competent facade, Amanda was afraid.

"You're safe now." Reluctant sympathy softened his voice. He ought to be delighted she'd been scared. Maybe that was what she needed to keep her from committing such idiocy.

But he wasn't. Instead, he had an equally idiotic urge to stop the car and take her in his arms. He clamped the steering wheel nearly as tightly as he was clamping his jaw.

"Thank you." She was staring down at the cell phone in her hand. At least she'd had sense enough to call for help. She shot a sideways glance at him. "How did you happen to come along at just the right moment?"

"No happen about it. I called C.J.'s number earlier this evening and reached her grandmother. She told me you were coming."

Amanda's expression said she didn't quite know which question to ask first. "Why did you call her? You said there was no story."

He was afraid she'd zero in on that. "I said

there was no story without more facts. That's what I was after."

"And that made you decide to come down here? Because you thought I might be in trouble or because you wanted to take over the interview?"

Just about any answer would only make the situation more uncomfortable. "I was late at the office. It was no trouble to swing by and make sure you were okay."

Which wasn't really an answer at all. Amanda probably knew he was late at the office every night. Probably thought he was a compulsive workaholic who had no life outside of work. She might just be right.

Amanda's brows knitted. "Were you going to come into the building?"

"Judging from C.J.'s grandmother's reaction to my call, I didn't think I'd be welcome. You have any luck?"

"Not much," she admitted. "But what were you doing? Waiting for me to come out?"

She was nothing if not persistent. It was a good quality in a reporter, but at the moment it annoyed the heck out of him.

"I was just pulling up when I saw you were alone on the curb." He ground out the words. "Speaking of which, where is your car?"

"I didn't want to leave it on the street, so—" She cut that off, consternation filling her face. "Good heavens, I forgot about my brother." She punched a button on the cell phone. Pressing it to her ear, she effectively ignored him.

He turned onto King Street and wondered where they were going. He had a vague sense she lived down in the historic district someplace, so he was probably headed in the right direction.

"Hugh? Listen, I got finished early, so I've already left. You don't need to—"

A male voice interrupted her, so loudly irate that Ross could hear it. He couldn't make out the words, but clearly Amanda was getting a much-needed earful from her brother.

"Yes, I know, but I wasn't in trouble—"

Annoyance prickled. She was sounding a lot more apologetic to the brother than she had to him.

"I'm telling you, I'm fine, so stop yelling. No, you don't need to get me. A…a friend is taking me home. Love you, okay?"

The resulting murmur sounded placated, if also a bit exasperated. Being Amanda's brother must be a full-time job, given her penchant for trouble.

She dropped the cell phone into her bag and brushed a wing of hair behind her ear. His hand tingled, as if he had touched the silky strand.

"You didn't fool him," he said, distracting himself.

"You mean about not being in trouble?" She blew out a breath. "It's tough to con Hugh, him being in law enforcement and all."

"To say nothing of knowing you since birth."

She grinned, the tension between them popping like a bubble. "That, too."

He'd probably be better off without being on the receiving end of too many of those impudent smiles. "One question? Where are we going?"

"Oh, sorry. I can call a taxi—"

"Just tell me." Maybe putting her in a cab was safer, given the level of attraction he felt in the close confines of the car, but...

She leaned forward, as if just noticing where they were. "It's not far, if you really don't mind driving me home. Just take the next left."

In a few minutes they were pulling to the curb of one of the narrow residential streets down near the Battery. "That's it?" He leaned across the front seat to peer through the window at the tiny house tucked between two graceful antebellum mansions.

"Small, but my very own." She opened the door, and the dome light showed him a faint embarrassment in her eyes. "Would you like to come in for a cup of coffee or an iced tea?"

He didn't want coffee, but he did want to see Amanda in her own setting and to say something to her where they could be face-to-face.

"I'd like to come in for a moment." He got out quickly, before she could think of a way to uninvite him, and walked around the car to join her on the curb.

Amanda pushed open the black wrought-iron gate that led to the tiny front garden of the equally tiny cottage. She hurried up the brick walk, pulling a ring of keys from her bag.

"My place was originally the gatehouse for that property."

She nodded to the house on the left. It loomed over its small neighbor, and he realized that the trim and paint color of the two was the same, despite the difference in their sizes.

"You were lucky to get something in the historic district." He'd been here long enough to know that finding an affordable place to live was a major preoccupation in Charleston.

"It belongs to a friend of a family friend," she said, opening the door and switching on lights. "Come in."

He stepped inside, feeling as if he had walked into a child's playhouse. At first sight the living room seemed cluttered to him, with chintz upholstered pieces, lacy curtains drawn back from plantation shutters, and photos covering every horizontal space, but after a moment's study he decided that *cozy* was a better word. It was a far cry from the sterile furnished apartment he occupied when he wasn't at the paper.

"It's nice," he said, feeling some comment was called for.

"All castoffs from the rest of the family. You wouldn't believe what my folks and my aunts and uncles have in their attics, to say nothing of Miz Callie." She tossed her handbag on a cherry drop-leaf table. "Now, what about that coffee?"

He could say yes. They'd sit close together on that chintz love seat... No, that would be a mistake. He might end up doing something he'd regret, like kissing her.

"No coffee." He took a step that closed the distance between them, seeing her eyes widen. "I came in to say something to you."

"W-what?"

He was close enough to hear the hitch in her breath, and that set his pulses racing. "You put yourself in danger tonight for a story. You will never do that again, or I will fire you. Understand?"

She nodded. Her lips trembled, drawing his attention to them.

He could sense how they'd feel under his—the shape of her mouth, the softness of her lips, the sweetness of her breath. He leaned toward her—

Back off, he commanded himself. That would be a mistake. Even if he weren't pursuing a story that might lead directly to her father, he couldn't get involved with someone who worked for him.

Amanda, despite her veneer of sophistication, was really a small-town girl at heart, giving up a promising job in Tampa to come home because of her family, from what he'd seen. A woman from a close-knit family like hers would believe in love and fidelity and happily-ever-after. All the things he dismissed as fiction.

She looked up at him from beneath her lashes, the glance tentative, questioning, as if she wondered what he was thinking. And he couldn't resist. He covered her lips with his.

The kiss was sweet…an almost platonic touch in comparison to some of the women he'd dated. But the impact rushed through him and headed straight for his heart, pummeling it unmercifully. He touched her arms, drawing her closer, and she leaned into his embrace with a little sigh that seemed to say she'd come home.

It was the sigh that brought him back to

himself. He couldn't do this. It was a mistake— a gigantic one.

It took more willpower than he'd known he possessed to pull away. Amanda's green eyes held a dazed expression that probably matched his own.

He had to search for the right words to say. "I'm sorry. I shouldn't have done that." He took a step back, feeling as if he'd left a part of himself behind.

Amanda shook her head, seeming to shake off the dream that held her dazed. "Don't apologize. You weren't the only one involved."

"No." He hadn't been, and that made things infinitely more complicated. "I'd better go." Before he made the situation even worse, if that was possible. "Good night, Amanda."

He turned and walked quickly away, because if he didn't, he wasn't sure how much more foolish he might have been.

The fact that Amanda was expected for supper at Mamma and Daddy's the night after her adventure at C.J.'s apartment was trouble on so many levels she wasn't sure how to count them. There was the fact of her having been stuck there, to begin with, and then there was that kiss, which she'd been trying all day to forget.

But the thing that made her chest tight and her

palms damp as she went up the walk to the front door was what she had seen when she'd climbed into Ross's car. She'd looked back, just a quick glance to be sure no one was coming after them.

The door to the bar had opened, and a man stepped out onto the sidewalk. Not just any man. The last man she'd expect to see in a place like that—her father.

She paused on the walk, ostensibly to admire her mamma's dahlias, blooming their hearts out along the veranda. But she wasn't really seeing them. She was seeing something furtive about that familiar figure in that place. Out of uniform.

Ask him. The voice of her conscience was blunt. *Just come right out and ask him.*

She could, of course. Make it light, as if it meant nothing at all. Which it didn't, she assured herself quickly.

That meant revealing her presence in that part of town, and Daddy wasn't going to be happy about that. But that wasn't really what held her back, and she knew it.

That odd interaction between her father and Ross lay at the bottom of her uneasiness. She'd tried again and again to tell herself that she'd imagined it. Unfortunately, she hadn't been able to make herself believe it.

Ross was still working on the Coast Guard story, even if he hadn't asked her for any more introductions. Maybe she'd already served his purpose when she'd introduced him to the family. She just didn't know what that purpose was.

She touched the brilliant face of an orange dahlia and straightened, heading for the door. She didn't know what she was going to do, but she'd best get inside before Mamma sent someone out to fetch her.

The brass knob was familiar to her hand, and the frosted glass sent back a dim reflection of her face. She turned the knob and walked inside, dropping her bag on the table under the mirror in the center hallway. Her heels clicked on the parquet floor.

"I'm here," she called. "Anybody home?"

"We're in here, sugar." Hugh's voice. If he'd told Mamma and Daddy what she'd got up to last night...

She walked into the parlor. Hugh's long legs were stretched out comfortably in front of him as he leaned back, looking practically boneless, on the couch. Annabel, in her usual jeans and T-shirt, perched on the arm next to him, her thick braid swinging across her shoulder.

Mamma was probably in the kitchen, but

Daddy sat bolt upright in his chair, hands planted firmly on his knees, looking as if he wanted to give someone a piece of his mind.

She exchanged a wordless glance with her twin. *Danger, danger...* Annabel didn't need to speak to convey the warning.

"What's this I hear about you gettin' into trouble last night, Amanda?"

She swung on Hugh. "You told."

He spread big hands wide. "I was makin' a joke of it, honest. I didn't know Daddy'd get so het up."

"Yeah, right. Tattletale."

"Right." Annabel weighed in instantly on her side. She swatted Hugh lightly on the head. "Troublemaker."

He grinned. "Daddy, the twins are picking on me."

"You ought to know better." Mamma appeared in the doorway, a wooden spoon in her hand, but it wasn't immediately clear whether she was talking to Amanda or Hugh. Or both.

"Do you need some help, Mamma?" She'd be just as glad to get into Mamma's less volatile company until Daddy forgot about this.

"No, no." Mamma waved the spoon. "It's just about ready, so don't settle down too much."

She vanished again.

Amanda turned to her sister, ready to change the subject with a question about Annabel's horses, but Daddy got in first.

"Amanda, where exactly were you last night?"

She pressed her lips together for an instant. This would be all right. She'd say where she'd been, and Daddy would comment on being in the same place, say he'd have come to her rescue if only he'd known, and her doubts would be wiped away.

"Down on Joslyn Street. The three hundred block. It's where my intern lives."

Where you were last night, Daddy. In a bar I'd never have expected you to touch with a ten-foot pole.

"It's not as bad as it sounds, I promise." Hugh sat up straight, bumping his legs on the coffee table. "I dropped her off, and I was coming back to get her."

Daddy frowned. "At least you two had that much sense. If I hadn't been stuck on base last night, I'd have taken her myself, if it was that important."

It struck her like a blow to the stomach. Daddy. Lying. She could hardly put the words together. That just didn't happen.

"Hugh took care of it," Annabel said, with the air of someone who didn't see what all the fuss was about.

"Actually, I didn't." Hugh's gaze met hers and then slid away. "Manda got done a little early, so a friend drove her home."

"Friend?" Daddy's voice cut like a knife. "What friend?"

She swallowed. "Not a friend, exactly. My boss. Ross Lockhart."

She saw the impact on her father. Saw it, saw him try to hide it. And knew that whatever had taken him to that bar last night, she couldn't ask him about it. She couldn't put him in a position where he'd lie to her again.

Amanda still worried about the situation the next evening when she walked the short two blocks to the home of Cyrus Mayhew. The *Bugle*'s publisher was having a party, and apparently the whole staff was invited.

That meant she'd be seeing Ross in a social setting. A business setting was bad enough. He'd been cool and distant at the office, as if to deny that their kiss had ever happened.

At least Ross had allowed her to do some minor investigating into the landlord situation. She'd discovered the owner was an absentee landlord, living on one of the gated barrier island communities off Beaufort, not here in Charleston at all.

She crossed the street toward Cyrus's place, cautious of the cobblestones of the historic district, never easy to navigate when wearing heels, and felt the breeze off the water. The Mayhew house proudly faced the Battery and Charleston harbor. Cyrus was fond of talking about the window glass that had broken during the siege of Fort Sumter, which was visible from his second-floor balcony during the day.

The wrought-iron gates stood hospitably open. She stepped into the walled garden where tiny white lights glistened in the trees, reflected from the surface of the oval pond and echoed the light summer colors of the women's dresses.

She hadn't gotten two feet when a waiter swept down on her with a tray of drinks, followed by a second with an array of canapés. She took an icy glass of lemonade and a mushroom tart, turned away and narrowly escaped the waving champagne glass of the *Bugle*'s society editor, Juliet Morrow.

"Evening, Amanda." Juliet beamed in her direction. Juliet did enjoy a party. "Be sure you get some of those crab turnovers, y'heah? They are superb."

"I'll do that." She bit into the flaky pastry of

the mushroom tart, feeling the flavors explode in her mouth. Cyrus had been a widower for years and showed no signs of wanting to change his marital status, to the despair of Charleston's female population, which thought he needed a hostess, at least. Instead, he employed the best caterer in town for his parties.

"Nice, isn't it?" Juliet's glass gestured to take in the garden, the caterer's people, even the graceful lines of the antebellum house. "Cyrus is lucky it didn't rain tonight. He wouldn't want this horde tramping on his Oriental carpets and puttin' their glasses down on his piecrust table."

"The air's heavy enough for a storm." Amanda quelled an inward shudder at the thought, never having managed to quite conquer a childish fear of thunderstorms. "I'm sure he'd be welcoming if we had to go inside." She glanced around, nodding to people she knew. "Where is he?"

Juliet lifted a perfectly plucked brow. "Our esteemed publisher? Or our hunky new managing editor?"

"Hunky?" She kept her voice level with an effort. She certainly didn't want to raise suspicions in Juliet's fertile imagination. "Really, Juliet, if you use that kind of language in your column, folks will think your beat is gossip, not society."

"This is just between you and me, darlin'." The society editor's smile held only a trace of malice. "You should know how attractive the man is, as much time as you've been spending with him. Tell me, what's really behind that gruff exterior?"

The memory of Ross's kiss flooded through her, and her cheeks heated. She could only hope the light was dim enough to hide it.

"Ah, I see I've hit a nerve." Juliet sounded as satisfied as a cat in the cream pitcher.

She should have known the woman could see in the dark, again like a cat. "Don't be ridiculous." Her voice was pitched higher than she wanted. "There's absolutely nothing between me and Ross Lockhart."

She turned, hoping to make a graceful exit from the conversation, and found Ross standing behind her. Juliet's soft laughter faded as the society editor walked away.

If there was a graceful way out of this situation, Amanda couldn't see it. "I'm sorry."

The words didn't seem to penetrate the stony mask that was Ross's face. Not much like the way he'd looked when he'd kissed her, was it?

"People are talking." He said the words as if they tasted bad.

"Just Juliet," she said quickly. "She's always imagining relationships that aren't there."

Except that something *was* there between them. One kiss didn't make a relationship, but it meant something, if only that he was attracted. As for her feelings—well, she wasn't going to explore that right now.

"It has to stop." That icy glare would make anyone quake.

A tiny flame of anger spurted up. She wasn't the one who'd initiated that kiss, after all. "Stopping gossip isn't in my job description."

One thing—she wouldn't have to worry about avoiding him. He'd never come near her after this. A quick retreat seemed in order, but before she could implement that, Cyrus swept down on them.

"Just the people I wanted to see." He put his arm around Amanda's shoulders, effectively cutting off her flight. "Now, I don't want to spend the evening talking business, but I do want to hear what the latest is on that troublesome landlord."

Amanda blinked. She hadn't realized Cyrus knew anything about that, given the reluctance with which Ross was pursuing the story.

"We've finished a lot of the background

research." Ross shifted into editor mode in an instant. "Jason Hardy owns several buildings in the area of C.J.'s apartment building, most of them in a questionable state. It looks as if he puts in barely enough repairs to keep on the right side of the housing inspectors, but he's skirting the line. I think we could make a case that he ought to be looked at more thoroughly."

"Maybe it's time we interviewed the man. Let him know the press is interested," Cyrus said.

The concerns C.J.'s grandmother had voiced echoed in Amanda's mind. "If you do that, he's going to think that C.J. is involved."

"Hardy lives down near Beaufort," Ross said, ignoring her as if she hadn't spoken. "I can go down and talk to him."

"Take Amanda with you." Cyrus squeezed her shoulders. "I want her involved."

Oh, no. That was what her heart was protesting. It was what Ross's expression said, as well.

"I don't think—" he began.

Cyrus cut that off with a wave of his hand. "It was her idea, after all."

"But if we interview him…" Neither man listened to her.

"Very well." Ross's voice was icy. "We'll go tomorrow."

Great. Ross didn't want this. She didn't want this. But they were both going to have to deal with it.

Chapter Eight

Amanda felt as if she'd been arguing with Ross all the way from Charleston to Beaufort. That wasn't quite true, of course. Most of the way she'd actually been arguing with herself.

How did I get into such a mess, Father? I thought this was going to help C.J., and instead it could cause her all kinds of heartache. I meant well.

That was a feeble excuse. How much of the world's trouble had been caused by people who were well-meaning? Too much, probably, and now she'd contributed her little bit.

Please, help me see what's best to do. Help me show Ross that we can't pursue the story if it's going to hurt more than it helps.

Was that the right thing to pray for? She slid a

sideways glance toward Ross, his face impassive behind his sunglasses as he concentrated on driving across the bridge from Beaufort to Lady's Island. Her chances of diverting him from a course he'd decided upon seemed slight, at the least.

She tried to still her doubts, staring out at the expanse of water, sky and islands. Beautiful, as always, but the dark clouds that hung on the horizon seemed to echo her mood.

I'll do my best to listen, Lord. Please show me the right thing to do for C.J. and her grand-mother. And for Daddy.

Her heart clenched into a tight, cold ball at the thought. Daddy. What was going on with him? What was Ross's interest in him? Neither of them was likely to tell her, but she couldn't just do nothing.

Guide me, Father. She came back, in the end, to the simplest words. *Guide me.*

Ross turned his head to look at her. She caught the movement in the periphery of her vision and tried to unclench the hands she'd had clasped in her lap.

"Is something wrong?" He sounded reluctant to ask the question, as if he wouldn't like the answer. Which he wouldn't.

"Just the same thing we've been talking about

for the past hour or so. I don't want C.J. and her grandmother to get hurt for the sake of a story."

Ross blew out an exasperated breath. "Maybe you should have been a social worker instead of a reporter. Our job is to get the story, that's all."

"No matter who gets hurt?"

His jaw clenched so hard that a tiny muscle twitched under the skin. "I'm not hurting anyone. The cheating landlord is the bad guy, remember?"

"I know. I agree." Why couldn't he understand this? "But if C.J. and her grandmother get kicked out of their building because of what we did, I'm not sure they're going to agree."

"May I remind you that you're the one who brought me the story?"

"That was before I'd talked to C.J.'s grandmother and realized what was at stake." She shouldn't have gone to him without more information.

"I don't want to see them get hurt," he said. "They ought to have an attorney represent them in this, but I don't suppose that's occurred to them."

"I've already taken care of that."

He lowered his sunglasses so that he could look over them at her face. "*You* took care of it?" He didn't sound as if he approved of that, either. "If it comes out that an employee of the *Bugle* is paying an attorney for the tenants, it will look as if we're manipulating the story."

"That's ridiculous. Anyway, I'm not paying anyone. My cousin's fiancé is an attorney, and he sometimes takes pro bono cases. Surely no one can make an argument out of that, just because I'm sort of related to him. I'm sort of related to half the county, if you go back far enough."

He glanced at her again, seeming to weigh what he saw there. "You really do go the extra mile, don't you?"

It almost sounded as if he cared. "I didn't think of it that way," she said slowly. "It just seems to me that people are more important than any story."

"That's a fatal mistake for a reporter." He snapped the words. Clearly he was back to being annoyed with her after what had seemed a moment's respite. "Besides, if this story pans out, it will benefit more people in the long run."

"Is that really why you're doing it?" The question was out before she thought that it might be offensive. She bit her lip. "I'm sorry. I didn't mean—"

"I know exactly what you meant." His voice turned icy. "I'm doing my job. If you can't do yours, maybe you're in the wrong line of work."

There didn't seem to be anything to say to that.

In fact, there didn't seem to be anything to say at all. As far as their values were concerned, she and Ross were miles apart.

Following the signs, they drove along the narrow road, salt marshes pressing close on either side, until they reached the gated community that occupied its own small island. To her surprise, Ross stopped before he reached the gatehouse, turning to zero in on her face.

"I'll focus my questions on the other buildings Hardy owns," he said abruptly. "This is about more than just the apartment house where C.J. and her grandmother live. That should keep him busy defending himself. There's no reason he'd assume C.J. was involved. If he does, between your lawyer friend and the newspaper's clout, we'll protect them."

Funny. He sounded as annoyed at himself for the concession as he was at her. His offer wasn't a great solution, but it looked as if it was the best she was going to get.

Ross kept what he hoped was a pleasant smile on his face as he surveyed Jason Hardy. The man had met them on the putting green that was apparently part of the landscaping of his luxurious property. The sprawling low country-style home was screened from other, equally expensive properties by the artful use of palmettos and crepe myrtles. Yes, Jason Hardy had it made, and he was clearly eager to show off.

"Had to have a putting green right here."

Hardy gestured expansively with a gloved hand. He couldn't be much over forty, tanned and groomed to perfection, from the carefully tousled hairstyle to the tips of his costly leather golf shoes.

"With the hours I work, it can be impossible to get in eighteen holes on a regular basis." He cast a look at the dark clouds massing on the horizon. "Wouldn't you know? I've cleared my schedule for the afternoon, and now there's a storm moving in."

"You don't find it inconvenient for your work to live clear out here?" Ross would gladly keep the man bragging about his success for a few minutes before letting him know that this interview wasn't going to be a puff piece about the rising young businessman.

"Cybercommuting," Hardy said quickly. "With the right use of technology, a busy man can be anywhere in the world in seconds."

"Is that right?" he murmured, as if he'd never heard of such a thing.

Amanda moved quietly around them, taking one photo after another. Without a word being spoken, she'd picked up on his idea. Show the man playing with his expensive toys while his tenants sweltered in the heat, his buildings falling down around them.

Amanda had good instincts. Unfortunately, she also had a soft heart that was going to get in her way when it came to being a decent reporter.

He was abruptly tired of buttering up this sleazeball. "So, your investments in slum housing in Charleston—are they doing well for you?"

Some of the bonhomie slid from Hardy's face. "I'm not sure what you mean. I am invested in some rental properties in the city, I believe."

"You're underestimating yourself, aren't you?"

He held out his hand. Amanda put the file folder into it without missing beat. He flipped the folder open and pretended to study it. Never mind that he'd committed its contents to memory. Hardy didn't need to know that.

"Let's see," he said. "That's twenty-six rental buildings all together, owned by you either directly or through a subsidiary company."

Hardy's eyes narrowed. "I guess that might be about right. It's a small part of my portfolio."

"And out of those twenty-six, there have been

two hundred and forty-seven complaints to the housing department. A hundred and ten investigations ensued. Fifty-four citations issued, ranging from broken heat pumps not fixed to questionable evictions to contaminated water."

Hardy held the golf club between them as if he felt the need for weapon. "What is all this? I thought you wanted to do a profile piece on me."

"A profile has to include both sides," he said gently. "Surely you realize that. Now, about the situation with the broken air-conditioning at…let me see…hmm, twenty of twenty-six buildings. That's a fairly large number, don't you think? A person might almost think the air conditioners in your buildings were deliberately put out of commission so you didn't have to pay those high electric bills this summer."

He let a smile play around his lips. There was nothing like it when an investigation came together—that wave of exhilaration knowing that the creep wasn't going to wiggle off the hook this time.

"You don't dare print that. It's speculation, that's all." Snatching his putters, Hardy stalked off the green. "Get off my property. You're not going to get away with ambushing me like this."

"Don't you want to give us a statement, Mr.

Hardy? I'm sure our readers would like to hear directly from you."

This story was small potatoes, he knew that. CNN wouldn't pick it up; there'd be no national interest. But for the first time in months, he felt like a reporter again.

Amanda moved around, the camera up to her face, snapping picture after picture. Hardy swung toward her, anger darkening his face.

"Stop taking pictures. Give me that." He grabbed for her.

Fury swept through Ross, but before he could move, Amanda slipped easily away from the man.

"You don't want to do that." Her voice was cool. "Think how bad it would look on the news if you assaulted a photographer."

Baffled, Hardy swung back to Ross. "Any of those pictures get in your second-rate rag, and I'll sue. I'm calling your publisher. We'll see about this."

Ross couldn't help but grin at the thought of Cyrus being intimidated. It would make Cyrus's week if Hardy actually called and threatened him.

"You do that, Mr. Hardy. I'm sure he'd like to hear from you." He gestured to Amanda and started walking toward the car. "Thanks for the interview."

* * *

Ross spent the first ten minutes of the drive back recording his impressions with the aid of a microcassette recorder. He was pleased with the way the interview had gone. Amanda could hear that in his voice.

And see it in his eyes, for that matter. As the sky continued to darken, he'd pulled off his sunglasses, allowing her to see the intent focus of his gaze.

He took pride in what he was doing. She might not like the "ambush" aspect of the interview, but she had to admit that probably nothing else would have worked with a man like Jason Hardy. She'd have been out of her depth if she'd been alone.

The thought was sobering. Maybe Ross was right. Maybe she wasn't meant to be a reporter, if that was what it took.

A few fat raindrops splattered on the windshield, and Ross clicked on the wipers. "It looks like Hardy isn't going to get in his golf game this afternoon."

"He's probably too busy anyway, what with needing to exert his influence to kill the story." A rumble of thunder sounded, and her hands clenched on her pant legs.

"Is something wrong?" He darted a look at her. The man had eyes that noticed every little thing.

"Nothing," she said, knowing it wasn't true. "I wanted to say…you handled him exactly right, even though I don't suppose much that he said will actually make it into the article."

"No, but it would be a shame to run the piece without having interviewed him."

"Do you really think he'll call Cyrus?"

Ross grinned. "I hope he does. Cyrus will have him for lunch, and probably get a quote out of it besides. But he won't. Hardy has undoubtedly called his attorney, who'll tell him he was an idiot for even talking to us."

"Hardy thought we were there to do a profile piece on him." That still bothered her.

"He's not smart enough to play with the big boys, then."

Obviously it didn't bother Ross.

"I'll tell you what's going to happen next," Ross said. "By the time we get back to the office, we'll have received a carefully worded statement from the lawyer, which we'll be obliged to print." He smiled thinly. "This is one place where your photographs will speak more loudly than his words, I think."

A clap of thunder punctuated his words, and then the storm was on them. Rain came down as if someone had emptied an immense bucket over their heads. In a moment, it was so dark it might have been dusk except when lightning forked toward the ground, illuminating everything in flickering bursts like a crazy series of still pictures. She couldn't keep a gasp from escaping.

"You really don't like storms, do you?" Ross said.

"Not much." She had to loosen tight lips to answer. "I'm such a wimp about it. When I was a kid, I used to hide in the closet. Or under the bed." She tried to smile. "No closets here, unfortunately. Just ignore me." She was thirty now, for pity's sake. It was time she acted like a grown-up.

"We can do better than that." He flicked the turn signal on. "Looks like a restaurant of some kind ahead, though I never really trust a restaurant whose sign just says 'eats.'"

"You don't need to…" she began, but he was already pulling into the crushed-shell parking lot.

"I'm getting hungry anyway. We'll get something to eat and wait out the storm." He pulled up next to the porch so that she could get from the car to the shelter of its roof in a quick step. "Ready?"

She nodded, took a shaky breath and opened the door.

Wind and rain struck her, but almost before she felt it, Ross had grabbed her arm and propelled her into the restaurant.

"Hey, folks." The grizzled elderly man behind the counter was the only occupant. "Y'all brought the rain with you."

"Not our idea," Ross said. "How about some coffee?"

"Comin' right up. You, missy?"

"Sweet tea, please." She headed for a booth on the inside wall, safely away from the windows, and slid in. She looked up at Ross in belated apology. "Sorry. Is this okay?"

He smiled, face relaxing. "Fine. Would you like me to ask him if he has a closet?"

The arrival of their drinks saved her from answering that. "What you folks want to eat?" The man, who was apparently server as well as cook, and maybe the owner, too, didn't seem inclined to offer a menu, but his apron was spotless and the aromas from the grill were all good. "The shrimp-burgers are nice today. And I got me some sweet potato fries."

"That sounds good to me." She'd learned, hitting some questionable roadside cafés coming and going from school in Columbia, that it was usually safest to order the day's special.

"A burger." Ross obviously didn't hold to that philosophy.

She lifted her brows after the man returned to his kitchen. "Don't care for the local cuisine?"

"Some things. What exactly is a shrimp-burger?"

"That depends on the cook. It might be a cold shrimp salad on a roll. Or it might be something like a crab cake, only made with shrimp. You take your chances."

"Thanks, but I'll just play it safe."

"You don't strike me as someone who plays safe." She took a sip of the tea. Sure enough, it was sweet enough to make teeth ache.

Ross frowned down at his coffee, as if he suspected an insult she hadn't intended. "You asked me something earlier," he said abruptly. "You asked if publishing the truth was my only reason for pursuing this story."

She didn't know what to say. Luckily she didn't have to, because he went on.

"I chase the story because that's who I am." He gave a wry smile. "An investigative reporter. This pretense of being an editor is wearing pretty thin. Cyrus knows that. That's why he pushed me to do this story."

"But if this job isn't what you wanted, why did you take it?"

If he hadn't, they'd never have met. She wasn't sure where that thought had come from, but she didn't like it.

"I didn't exactly have a lot of choices." His lips pressed together for an instant. "You must know what happened to me in D.C. Big story…made the wire services and the television talk shows. It's too bad I didn't write it."

"I know what people said about what happened," she said carefully. "I don't know if that's the truth."

"The truth can be an elusive thing."

Ross stared at the checked oilcloth that covered the tabletop, looking as if he didn't see it. Rain clattered against the tin roof, making so much noise that it would be impossible for anyone else to hear them, even if anyone had been there.

Would he go on or was that all he was willing to say, at least to her?

"I was after the story of my career." He seemed to force the words out. "I'd been following leads on congressional misdeeds for a couple of weeks. That was a shade on the ironic side for me."

"Because your father was a congressman." That fact had received a lot of play in the reporting, she remembered.

"Right." Tension cut deep lines in his face. "I

wasn't getting very far. I heard plenty of rumors that a particular popular congressman was letting special interests line his pockets, but no way to prove it. Then I ran into a old buddy of mine from law school. When he heard what I was working on, he said maybe he could help."

He began playing with his spoon, turning it over and over in his fingers.

"Vince was a lobbyist. People talked to him who would never talk to a reporter. Anyway, he came back to me in a couple of days. Said he'd found someone who could deliver the goods—photos, statements, everything. For a price, of course." The spoon flipped from his fingers to land on the table, and he picked it up again. "The paper was willing to spring for it. The editor was salivating at the idea. Pushed me to go ahead. Move fast, before someone else got onto it."

She could see where this was headed, and she hurt for him. "Your friend set you up."

"They did a great job. It was like something out of Woodward and Bernstein, right down to the meet-in-a-parking-garage. I turned over the money, the guy turned over the pictures, the paper rushed into print the next day. And then found out we'd been suckered when the whole story was easily disproved by the congressmen's staff." He shrugged. "Long story short, someone had to take the fall for it. I was the one whose byline was on the story."

Without thinking, just needing to comfort, she put her hand over his. "I'm so sorry. If he hadn't been your friend…"

"If he hadn't been my friend, I wouldn't have fallen for it so easily. Even so, I should have taken a few more days to check it out. I didn't. My fault." His hand turned, and he clasped her fingers.

"It's not a bad thing to trust a friend. Or to want to succeed." She discovered that her breath was playing tricks on her…catching in her throat just because he was touching her that way.

He folded his other hand over hers, so that hers was enclosed in his warm grip. His fingertips stroked the inside of her wrist almost absently, as if he didn't realize he was doing it, but took some comfort from the touch.

"I had everything going for me then. The right connections, the right job, a fast track to the top. And then it was gone in an instant, and I was a pariah. No one in Washington wanted to speak to me."

"They judged you without bothering to find out the truth." Guilt pierced her heart. Hadn't she done the same when she'd first heard the story?

Forgive me, Lord. I was so quick to judge. I'm ashamed of myself. I didn't think I was like that.

"If not for Cyrus's eccentric charity, I'd be looking for a new profession."

"You want your career back." She said what she sensed under his words.

"Of course I want it back." His grip tightened almost painfully. "All I need is one story big enough to hit nationally. If I get that, someone will take a chance on me. I can get back to a national market."

All he wanted was to leave here. The thought made a hollow spot in her heart.

She tried to rally. Naturally he'd want to get back to Washington. With his family background, he'd probably dreamed all his life of working there.

"Your family…" She let that trail off, not sure what she wanted to say.

He let go of her hands, and she was cold without his touch. His face hardened into a mask to shield his feelings.

"You know what the motto of my family was? Never embarrass your father. And I never did, until I really did it up right, with stories in every major daily."

The bitterness in his voice shook her. "But he must have understood that it wasn't your fault."

"He must?" His ironic expression mocked her words. "I don't know, because he was never willing to talk to me about it. He sent a message via one of his aides. A check, actually, accompanied by the suggestion that a new life somewhere far away might be a good idea."

The pain she felt for him was a knife in her heart. If she lived to be a hundred, she could never understand a parent acting like that. "I'm sorry." It came out as a whisper, earning her one of his sardonic smiles.

"Don't look so tragic, Amanda. It wasn't exactly a surprise. I knew what to expect from him."

That made it all the sadder, but she didn't suppose she'd better say that to him.

She'd add that to the other thing she'd never say to him. That she'd realized, while he was holding her hands and telling her his private grief, how much she cared for him. Cared deeply.

Because she cared, she wanted him to have what he wanted, even if that meant she'd lose him.

You can't lose what you've never had, she reminded herself. Somehow that didn't comfort her. When—not if, when—Ross left, he'd take a piece of her heart with him.

Chapter Nine

Amanda consistently turned to two people when she needed to talk—one was Miz Callie, the other was her twin. Mamma sometimes complained about that, but in a good-natured way. She said she'd get her own back when Amanda and Annabel had daughters, and they turned to her.

"If I'd known you were going to put me to work, I'd have gone to see Miz Callie today," Amanda said in mock complaint.

She scooped a bucket of feed from the bin her sister indicated.

"Miz Callie would give you cookies and sympathy," Annabel retorted. "Since you came here, you must need something else. Or you know what Miz Callie would say, and you want a different opinion."

"Who made you so smart? You're the kid sister, remember?"

"Only by twenty minutes."

The familiar banter with her twin was comforting. She had tight relationships with her brothers, but that was nothing like the bond with Annabel. Her twin was almost her other half.

She followed Annabel down the row of stalls. Her sister's menagerie seemed to have grown a little each time Amanda came to the farm Annabel owned out in the country north of Mount Pleasant. Her latest addition was a small gray donkey.

Amanda stopped at his pen and poured the feed into the bucket. "What's this guy's name?" She reached out to pet the donkey, but he yanked his head away, showing the whites of his eyes.

"Toby." Annabel leaned against the stall bar, frowning a little when she looked at the donkey. "He's still pretty skittish, I'm afraid. More so than I imagined he'd be. But you'll be okay, won't you, Toby? You just need a little time to learn you can trust us."

The donkey, apparently reassured by the love he heard in Annabel's soft drawl, edged his way back to the feed bucket and began to eat, his eyes still rolling at the slightest move.

"He was treated badly." Now that he was close, Amanda could see the scars.

Annabel just nodded. She didn't like to talk about the things that had happened to the animals she sheltered, but every vet and animal control agent in the county knew he or she could count on Annabel to take in their worst cases.

"The vet says he's healing okay, but the scars go deeper than the physical."

Amanda found those words echoing in her mind as she followed Annabel through the chores. Some scars did go deep. The story Ross had told her—how much was he still hurting from the betrayal of his friend? His parents, too, had let him down, as had the employer who hadn't trusted him enough to look for the truth.

Ross had let her see more deeply into his heart than she'd dreamed he would. She wanted to help him, but for the first time in her life, she doubted her ability.

Annabel let her alone, maybe knowing she needed time. Finally, when they leaned on the pasture fence admiring the horses that stood in the shade of the live oak, Annabel turned, eyebrows lifting.

Amanda knew that expression. After all, she had one exactly like it. Looking at Annabel was like looking in a mirror, aside from minor differences in hairstyle and clothes. Her sister was waiting to know why she was here today.

"It's complicated," she said, as if Annabel had asked the question aloud. She propped a sneaker on the fence slat and frowned down at the stain on the toe. Her own fault—she knew better than to wear new sneakers to the farm.

Her sister nodded. "It usually is. Is this about your boss?"

She didn't bother asking how Annabel knew. Twins just did. "Ross is different from anyone else I've ever…well, cared about."

She couldn't say they were in a relationship, because they weren't. But there was that kiss. And the way he'd confided in her. That meant something, didn't it?

"He's not your usual lost soul, that's for sure." Annabel leaned against the fence, absently adjusting her ball cap to keep the sun out of her eyes.

"Come on. I don't *always* go for needy guys, do I?" That was the family's running commentary on the guys she dated. Annabel collected stray animals; Amanda collected stray people.

"Pretty much."

"Well, maybe so. Anyway, Ross is different." He needed healing, just like the creatures who found their way to Annabel's care, but he wouldn't admit that easily. "I'm not even sure how it happened, but I care."

Love? She wasn't going to say love, not yet.

"What about him?"

"I don't know. He's attracted, but it's complicated. I mean, he's my boss, for one thing. And besides that…"

She couldn't tell even Annabel what Ross had told her. That shook her. She'd always been able to tell Annabel everything.

"Besides, I don't think he's going to be around that long. His goal is to get back to a big metropolitan market. Charleston is just a stepping stone for him."

"Honey, don't go falling in love with a man who'll take you away from us. I don't want to go chasing all over the country every time I need some twin talk." Annabel's tone was light, but her eyes were serious.

"It's not just that." She blew out a breath. "Ross wants his career back, and I'm not sure what he'd do to get it."

That was the crux of the matter, she realized. As usual, talking to Annabel had made things clear to her.

Ross had shown her pieces of himself, and she

had come to understand what drove him. But she still didn't know who he was, soul deep. She didn't know what he'd sacrifice to get back the life he felt had been stolen from him.

"Manda…" Annabel touched her hand lightly. "Be careful, okay?" Her tone was troubled. "I don't want to see you get hurt by caring for someone who isn't going to put you first."

The words weighed on her. Annabel knew what that was like, and Amanda had gone through that hurt with her. She didn't want to open herself up to that.

"I'll try." Her throat tightened. "But I'm afraid it might already be too late."

This trip to the Coast Guard Base was probably a waste of time, but Ross felt stuck with it. Impatience prickled along his nerves as he followed Amanda through the check-in procedure and back outside again.

He should be following up on another interview with a local supplier to the base, not walking around like a sightseer. And the slumlord story waited on just a few more follow-up questions. He'd assigned that to Jim Redfern, knowing the veteran reporter would cover all the angles.

But he knew himself well enough to recognize

the reluctance with which he'd let go of that story. He'd told Amanda that he was kidding himself, playing at being an editor instead of an investigative reporter, and he hadn't even known that until the words came out of his mouth.

He let his gaze linger on Amanda. She walked slightly in front of him with that quick, graceful stride, her silky hair ruffling in the breeze off the water. An enormous pair of sunglasses hid her eyes, but couldn't mask the eagerness in her expression at the thought of showing him something more about the service that was so important to her family.

He seemed to see her again across the table from him in that roadside restaurant, leaning toward him, her face filled with concern. Was that concern what had prompted those confidences? He certainly hadn't planned on telling her any of that, but it had spilled out. He'd been like the mail room kid, leaning on her desk to share his dreams.

That shouldn't happen again. She was too caring, and he found it too easy to respond to that.

Besides, the more involved he became in her life, the more it would hurt her if her father ended up the subject of a front-page exposé.

"Adam's due to meet us in a couple of minutes." Amanda stopped in the shade of one of the white buildings that dotted the area. "We may as well wait here for him."

He nodded, trying to block distractions from his mind. He'd be better off to focus on the moment—convince himself that he really was here to develop a story on the base. From what he'd seen of Adam Bodine, there was a sharp mind behind that genial exterior. It wouldn't do to make him suspicious of Ross's motives.

Leaning against the wall, he watched the play of light and shadow on Amanda's delicate features. Actually, maybe that wasn't a very good idea, either.

"Have you come here often?" He asked the question at random, trying to distract himself.

She turned toward him, her face lighting with eagerness. "This has always been one of my favorite places, since I was a kid. Even when my daddy was assigned elsewhere, there always seemed to be a Bodine who was posted here."

"I'm surprised you didn't go into the Coast Guard, too, then." If she had, he'd probably never have met her. That thought troubled him more than it should.

She tilted her head, considering. "I guess it is odd, but I never even thought of it. I always knew I'd be a writer of some sort."

"Why journalism, instead of fiction?"

"I guess I've always been more interested in real people than imaginary ones."

"That's probably the secret to your popularity at the paper. Everyone wants to talk to you." Did that sound as if he was envious? Nonsense. It didn't matter to him how many admirers Amanda had.

He could see her eyes crinkle at that, even with the dark glasses she wore. "Sometimes what they want is to complain."

"About what?" Then he caught on. "About their hard-hearted new boss, I suppose."

"Oh, they have some better adjectives than that," she assured him.

"I can imagine." He found he was leaning a little closer, drawn into Amanda's orbit despite his best intentions. "Would you care to share some?"

Her lips pursed. "My mamma taught me not to use language like that."

He quelled a ridiculous urge to kiss those lips right here in public. Maybe it was just as well that her cousin Adam was striding toward them along the walk, looking ready for anything in his blue shirt and pants, a blue ball cap with the Coast Guard emblem square on his head.

"Hey, Manda. Ross. Sorry to keep you waiting." Adam shook hands with him and gave Amanda a quick hug. "I had to clear something up, but now I'm all yours. What would you like to see first?"

"Let's go down to the docks," Amanda suggested.

Ross nodded. It didn't matter what they saw today, since that wasn't the story he was after, but he'd play along.

They started along the walk, and Adam fell into step with him. "What specifically is the aim of your article? If I knew that, I could tailor the tour to it."

The aim of my article is to expose somebody, maybe somebody named Bodine, as crooked. No, he couldn't say that.

"A general look at the different facets of your work," he said instead. "I'm not sure exactly what we'll be using in the finished series of articles, but it's all new to me."

"There's Win," Amanda said. She nodded toward a group of men and women jogging past.

One broke away and jogged toward them. Ross recognized the Bodine Amanda had pointed out as a rescue swimmer at the party. Probably a year or two younger than Amanda, Win Bodine had the long, lithe lines and the upper-body strength of a swimmer combined with the spark of a daredevil in his eyes. He stopped beside them, still jogging.

"Hey, how're you doing? Adam said you'd be comin' by today. I'll tell you all about being a rescue swimmer, if you want."

"What's to tell? You just have to jump out of a helicopter into the ocean now and then. Easy enough for someone who's half fish and half seagull." Adam's tone made it clear that this was familiar territory for the cousins.

"You're just jealous because women are more impressed by my job than yours." Win continued to jog with the easy manner of someone who probably wasn't even aware that he was doing it.

"Is that why you struck out and had to spend Saturday night playing air hockey at my place?"

The teasing was the kind that went on between men who knew each other to the bone. In this case, probably literally from birth. Amanda looked on with an indulgent smile.

He tried to ignore a stab of pure envy. The Bodines didn't know how lucky they were. Probably didn't even realize some people didn't have that kind of family bond.

Would that bond be enough to hold them

together if Brett Bodine ended up convicted of extorting bribes? That was an ugly thought, and he didn't have a clue as to the answer.

"Your crew is getting away from you," Amanda pointed out, nodding to the group Win had been jogging with. "You two can save your macho teasing for another time."

Win laughed. "And I've got just the time. Miz Callie called, and she's fixing to cook up a ton of steamed shrimp and some pecan pie tomorrow night. She said to pass it along to you if I saw you. You, too, Ross. She'll give you a call herself, but don't you disappoint her, now."

He waved, breaking into a run toward his group, who jogged in place waiting for him, yelling out a few gratuitous insults as they did.

"Sounds like some good eating," Adam said. "You're coming, aren't you, Ross?"

He should make some excuse. He shouldn't socialize with people who were going to be slammed if the story broke the way he thought it was going to. But Amanda was looking at him with obvious pleasure at the prospect, and he discovered he loved seeing that look in her eyes.

He shouldn't, but he was going to, and he'd just have to deal with the consequences.

"Sounds good," he said. "I'll be there if I can."

Adam gave a quick nod. "Okay. So, what do you want to see first?"

"You know perfectly well where you want to start," Amanda said. "Go ahead, show us the cutters and patrol boats."

"Well, since you insist."

Ross followed the two of them, letting the easy banter between the cousins flow over him.

When they reached the docks, Adam stopped at a businesslike white-and-orange boat with an enclosed cabin. "Here she is. My patrol boat—home away from home."

"Your first love," Amanda teased.

"Maybe that, too."

Amanda turned at a hail from farther along the dock, obviously seeing someone she knew, and scurried off to talk to two young men in Coast Guard blue.

"Is there anyplace in Charleston where Amanda doesn't have friends?"

"Nope. That's our Amanda." Adam's open face filled with affection as he watched his cousin. "She's always been everyone's friend and confidante. There are times when I wish she wasn't quite so trusting."

Ross stiffened. Was that aimed at him? "That's a good quality, isn't it?"

Now the look Adam turned on him was distinctly serious. "I wouldn't change her if I could. But she does lead with her heart. I wouldn't want her to get hurt."

"Is that a warning?" His jaw tightened. Adam couldn't know there was anything more than a professional relationship between them.

"Well, now, I wouldn't say that. I guess the days are long past when the Bodine boys would threaten to land hard on anyone who messed with one of them. Just consider it a bit of friendly advice. Bodines stick together, no matter what."

Amanda rejoined them, giving him no opportunity to say more, but his mind spun with the implications of Adam's words. Was that just cousinly protectiveness? Or did Adam know something about the investigation?

How could he? But Ross couldn't shake the suspicion that something more was going on than met the eye.

Amanda marched toward Ross's office that afternoon, seething. She'd come back to the newsroom from a late lunch satisfied that Ross had been shown the best of Coast Guard. That surely he must feel the same patriotic pride that she did after spending time with the people of Coast Guard Base Charleston.

Jim Redfern had been waiting for her, his normally dour face wearing even deeper grooves than usual. C.J. wasn't there, because she'd learned that Ross planned to use her and her grandmother as examples in the slumlord story. She'd walked out.

Crusading spirit carrying her along, Amanda rapped sharply on the door frame of Ross's office and walked in without waiting for an invitation.

Ross, telephone to his ear, lifted level brows at her impetuous entrance and held up one hand, palm out, to stop her. The gesture just added fuel to the flame.

She stalked across the office, frowning at the large-scale map of Charleston that filled most of one wall. Ross faced it while sitting at his desk, while behind him stretched a whiteboard, a corkboard and a flow chart showing what everyone on the staff was working on. That was it. There wasn't a single personal item on the walls.

Or on the desk. Ross was, as far as his office was concerned, a man without personal connections at all.

The reminder of what he'd shown her of himself cooled her anger slightly. Just in time, as he hung up the phone, dropped the pen with which he'd been making notes, and turned his frown on her.

"What?"

"I understand from Jim that you plan to use C.J. and her grandmother as examples in the story about Hardy." She tried for cool and collected. They were two professionals discussing a problem—that was all.

The small muscles around his mouth compressed. "That's right."

"You can't do that," she said flatly, her air of detachment fizzling away as quickly as it had come. "I told you how they felt about it."

He shoved his chair back, putting a little more distance between them. "This is about reporting a story, Amanda. Not about catering to somebody's feelings."

"It's not a question of catering to someone's feelings, as you so nicely put it." She'd find it so much easier to argue with him if she weren't so aware of his every movement—of the way his long fingers tightened around the chair arm, of the narrowing of his eyes at her defiance. She grasped after the detachment she'd lost. "All I'm saying is that surely we can run the story without hurting the individual."

He made an impatient, chopping motion with his right hand. "A dry recital of facts won't interest the reader or sell papers. We need the human element."

"Even if it hurts the very people you're trying to help?"

"Newspapers are in the business of reporting the news, not helping people, as I've told you repeatedly. The story serves the greater good."

He blew out an exasperated breath, as if he tired of having the same argument with her, reminding her of that moment when he'd said that if she wanted to help people, she should go into social work.

He couldn't really be that hardened, could he? Her heart twisted. This would be so much easier if she didn't know what was behind the cynical attitude. If she didn't care so much that he get what he longed for.

A memory flashed into her mind. Miz Callie, comforting her in the midst of some teenage crisis of the heart.

I love him, she'd wailed. Miz Callie's reply had contained a world of wisdom. *Then you'll want him to have his heart's desire, child. That's what loving is, even when it hurts.*

His taut posture eased a little, as if her silence meant the battle was won.

"What about C.J.?" If she couldn't fight him for herself, she could for someone else.

"What about her?"

"She found out. She's left."

Something flickered in his eyes at that. He hadn't known, and it mattered to him. She leaned toward him, hands on the edge of his desk, pressing the point home.

"This isn't just some faceless person you're throwing under the bus for the sake of a story. This is C.J. This internship was supposed to help her, not make her life more difficult. Surely there's a way to write a story with an impact that doesn't hurt her."

For a moment the silence stretched between them, his gaze fixed on her face. Then…

"You write it," he said abruptly.

"What?" She stepped back, not sure what he meant.

"You work with Jim. You do the human interest aspect of the story. Get it from C.J. or get it from someone else, but get it."

It was a challenge. Did he think she couldn't rise to it? If so, he'd be disappointed.

She tried not to let satisfaction tinge her smile or her voice.

"Thank you, Ross. I won't disappoint you."

To her surprise, his lips twitched slightly. "You madden, annoy, bemuse and surprise me, Amanda. But you never disappoint."

Before she could respond, he'd turned back to his computer, giving her a chance to get out of his office, hoping he hadn't noticed the stunned look on her face at his words.

Chapter Ten

Tradition had it that Charleston's Market had been on the same spot for a couple of centuries. Amanda didn't find that hard to believe as she stepped into the welcome shade under the roof that stretched along the aptly named Market Street almost to the old Customs House. Under its shelter, folks sold just about everything imaginable, with the emphasis on goods that would attract the tourists that flooded the historic district.

Amanda made her way along the crowded aisle, nodding to a few of the sweetgrass basket weavers she'd interviewed over the past couple of months for the story that might never see the light of day. And speaking of stories that might fail, she was here to find a way of convincing C.J. and her grandmother to cooperate.

If they didn't get on board with the story, she'd have to find someone else who would, and the clock was ticking. She couldn't kid herself that Ross would hold the article for her.

So she'd do this because she had to, and she'd show Ross in the process that it wasn't necessary to sacrifice someone for the sake of a story.

He should know that. He'd been the one sacrificed himself. Somehow that had only made him more determined to get back on top. Her heart twisted a little at the thought.

Please, Lord... She stopped, not even sure how to pray in this situation. *I want what's best for Ross. And for C.J. and her grandmother. Please show me what that is. Amen.*

She stepped into a band of sunlight where the roofs didn't quite meet, and then back into the shadows again. There, right in front of her, was another sweetgrass basket stand. C.J.'s grandmother sat weaving, her gaze moving over the people who passed by. When she came to Amanda, she made no sign of recognition at all.

C.J., manning the counter, hadn't mastered that impassive stare. Her brows lowered, her mouth tightened. If she'd had something in her hands, she just might have thrown it.

"C.J.—"

"Forget it. I got nothin' to say to you."

Amanda hesitated, her throat tight. "I think you have a lot that you'd like to say to me. You're angry."

"You just bet I'm angry." C.J.'s hands gripped the rough edge of the wooden counter on which the baskets were displayed. "You acted like you were my friend. But you just wanted to use me for a stupid article in the paper." Her lips twisted. "Your big chance to write somethin' besides dog shows, wasn't it?"

That hit too close to home. Hadn't that been in her mind the evening she'd gone to C.J.'s apartment?

"I wanted to write something more important. You know that. But not at the cost of hurting you." She pressed her fingers against the counter, willing C.J. to listen. To understand. "I only mentioned the situation to Mr. Lockhart because I thought the paper might help you."

"Fat lotta help that's going to be, when he prints our names and the landlord comes down on us for telling you. How's it help us when we're out on the street? Like my grandma says, none of the neighbors are fool enough to stick their necks out and talk to you."

"It's not just a question of you and your neighbors," Amanda said. The grandmother was listening, even if she made no sign of it. This argument was for her, as well as C.J. "We looked into Mr. Hardy's business dealings. He owns a number of buildings in your area, and he handles them all in the same way. There are a lot of people besides you and your grandmother hurting because of that man, and he gets away with it because everyone's afraid to complain."

C.J. looked taken aback at that, but then she shook her head. "Well, go get some of them to be in your story, and leave us alone."

"I could." *Maybe, if I had the time.* "But you're the one my attorney friend offered to help. And I want to do the story about you, because I believed you're a fighter. Maybe I was wrong."

"Don't you say that." C.J.'s grandmother rose, dropping the half-made basket onto her worktable. She held her head as proudly as if it bore a crown. "This grandchild of mine sure enough is a fighter."

"Leave it be, Gran." C.J. took her arm, urging her back to her seat. "We're better off not having anything to do with her. You were right."

Mrs. Carrey shook her off. "Why?" she demanded. "Why you giving in so easy on this? You were all het up about it before I talked you out of it."

"For you." C.J. put her arm gently around the older woman. "You took care of me all these years. Now's my turn to take care of you."

The woman reached up slowly, laying a worn, wrinkled hand on C.J.'s smooth cheek. She shook her head, tears gleaming suddenly in her eyes. Without looking at Amanda, she spoke.

"Miz Bodine, your grandmamma is a strong woman, I know."

Amanda thought of Miz Callie, determined to brave the disapproval of her entire community in order to right a decades-old wrong. Tears filled her eyes. "Yes, ma'am, she is a strong woman."

The woman nodded slowly. She patted C.J.'s cheek. "That's what I want this grandchild of mine to think about me."

"Gran, I do," C.J. protested. "You're the bravest woman I ever knew. I just think you shouldn't have to fight anymore."

Mrs. Carrey looked over C.J.'s shoulder to meet Amanda's gaze. "This child's something special, you know that? She's the only one of the family who has the brains and the gumption to make something of herself, and here I was, telling her to be afraid. Not to fight. I'm ashamed of myself."

"But Gran…"

"No buts." She gave C.J. a smile so full of love that it took Amanda's breath away. "We aren't quitters. We're fighters. We'll show that *t'ief* something." She shot a glance at Amanda. "You know what *t'ief* means?"

"Yes, ma'am, I do." She couldn't help the grin that spread over her face. The Gullah expression she'd applied to Mr. Hardy was only too appropriate. A thief.

"Well, that's what he is, and I guess your story is gonna show that to the world." She shoved the counter to make room for Amanda to squeeze through. "You come back here and let's get started."

Amanda rinsed dinner plates that evening while Miz Callie cut generous slices of pecan pie for dessert. Miz Callie's shrimp feast had been a small party by Bodine family standards. She'd invited only Hugh, Win, Adam and Georgia, along with Georgia's fiancé, Matt, and his little girl. And Ross.

Amanda stacked the plates and turned to her grandmother. "So, Miz Callie, you want to tell me why you invited Ross to this particular little group?"

"Well, now, I just thought it'd be a bit easier

to get acquainted without the whole kit and caboodle of Bodines here tonight. So I invited the ones I thought he'd enjoy getting together with."

Amanda leaned against the counter, surveying her grandmother. Something about that innocent blue-eyed gaze made her suspicious. "Are you sure that's all?"

Miz Callie's lips twitched. "Well, I did notice a little bit of tension between him and your daddy, so I thought we'd do without your folks tonight. I always thought Brett would take on at the idea of his baby girls getting serious about anybody."

Her cheeks warmed. "We're not… I mean I don't think…"

Might as well give up on that sentence. She didn't think her romantic attachment, or lack of one, had anything to do with Daddy's attitude, but maybe it was better not to trouble Miz Callie with that.

Her grandmother gave her a probing stare. "Is that what has you so distracted tonight, child?"

Distracted? Who, her? She'd fully expected Ross to make some excuse to get out of this dinner tonight, given how exasperating he seemed to find her lately. But there he was, sitting next to her through dinner, his arm brushing hers each time he moved, sending her senses shivering.

"I'm not distracted. Well, I guess I'm a little worried."

"About what?" Miz Callie paused in the act of putting pie on a tray, apparently ready to keep everyone waiting for their dessert to hear what troubled her.

"I'm just…" She tried to frame her worries in a coherent way. Her concerns about C.J. and her grandmother, her worries about the unaccountable animosity between Daddy and Ross…maybe they all amounted to the same kind of fear.

"I'm worried about whether I'm doing the right thing in a couple of situations," she said finally. That pretty much covered it.

"Have you prayed about this?" That would always be Miz Callie's first response to trouble.

"Yes. But probably not enough."

Miz Callie smiled. "You know perfectly well, Manda, that you rush right into doing things because they're good, and that's a beautiful quality. But maybe you need to take time to find out if they're the good things God has in mind for you."

That was a complicated and sobering thought. Caring about Ross was good, but was it good for her? She didn't know.

"Sometimes it's hard to know what God's plan is, even when I'm trying to pay attention."

"I know what you mean." Miz Callie patted her cheek, and she flashed back to C.J.'s grandmother doing the same thing to her. "I find the more I'm trying to steep myself in prayer and God's word, the easier it is to see what's right. Just wait and trust."

"I'll try." She blinked back tears. "Thank you, Miz Callie. You're a wise woman." If she and C.J. turned out half as well as their grandmothers, they'd be doing fine.

"Go on with you." Miz Callie waved away the compliment. "You take that coffee in before they think we've forgotten them."

But when she got into the dining room with the coffee service, no one seemed to be missing her. Instead, they were grouped around Ross, looking at some papers on the table in front of him.

Georgia waved a sheet of paper at her, her cheeks pink with excitement. "Manda, just look what Ross found for us. Miz Callie, look."

Miz Callie set down the tray of pie and pulled glasses from her pocket to perch them on her nose. "What is it?"

"Ross got us enlistment records for the month of August of '42 from every recruitment center in a hundred-mile radius of Charleston." Adam sent Amanda a questioning look. "I didn't realize he was in on our little hunt."

"I explained that we're trying to find out what happened to a relative of Miz Callie's," she said quickly, a note of warning in her voice. "He had some helpful suggestions, but I didn't know about this."

Why on earth had Ross pursued the matter on his own? She'd have expected him to forget it the instant they'd finished talking about it.

Faint embarrassment showed in Ross's expression when he shrugged. "It's no big deal. Amanda and I talked about how you'd track someone who'd enlisted under a false name under those circumstances, and I just got curious. I contacted a researcher I used to use in D.C., and he was able to locate the records for the centers that seemed the most likely."

Miz Callie sat down, seeming to realize all of a sudden what this might mean. "Goodness gracious." She pulled the papers toward her. "If Ned is in here—well, I guess we just have to hope he used a name that meant something. If he did, maybe I'll know it when I see it." She looked at Ross. "I purely don't know how to thank you. Words just aren't enough."

"Thanks aren't necessary," Ross said quickly. He was clearly embarrassed at being the center of so much appreciation. "Really, it was nothing."

"It was a kind deed," Miz Callie said, her voice firm as she reached out to clasp his hand. "Don't you ever go discounting the power of a kind deed."

Ross clasped Miz Callie's fine-boned hand in his, and Amanda wondered if he was thinking of his own grandmother and what he'd said about her that first time he'd given her a glimpse of the man behind the mask.

"It was my pleasure to help you," he said.

And her heart turned over, seeming to unfold like a flower.

I love him, she thought, surprised. *I love him.*

Ross leaned on the deck railing, looking out at the ocean that moved softly in the dark, lit only where the moon traced a shimmering pathway on the water. He heard the door open and close behind him and knew without looking that it was Amanda.

"They're still at it," she said, coming to lean on the railing next to him. Her arm brushed his, sending a flare of awareness through him.

Where had it come from, this instinctive reaction to Amanda? He hadn't expected it or even necessarily welcomed it, but there it was. If she was anywhere within range, he knew where. If she touched him, no matter how impersonally, he felt it to the marrow of his bones.

"This hunt of yours seems important to them."

"It'll make Miz Callie happy. She's frustrated at the idea of never knowing what happened to Ned."

She was editing what she told him, and he seemed to know that, also by instinct. "I heard someone say he was a Bodine. I thought he was a relative of your grandmother's."

"He was Granddad's older brother," she said. "There was a family quarrel, and he just disappeared. She feels as if she has to know."

He suspected that still wasn't the whole story, but that didn't seem to matter. At the moment nothing seemed to except being here with Amanda.

He knew all the reasons why this was a bad idea. He'd listed them to himself plenty of times. But for once his intellect and his feelings were not working in tandem.

"Take a walk on the beach?" he asked abruptly.

"Sure thing." She lifted her head, as if sniffing the breeze. "The wind's off the ocean, so the bugs shouldn't be biting too badly."

"That makes sense, I guess, but every time you drop a little bit of nature lore, it confuses me." He followed her down the stairs.

"Why?" She stopped at the bottom to wait for him, her face a pale oval in the dim light.

"Out here, you're nature girl in your shorts and T-shirts, knowing all about the tides and the flora and fauna. Back in the office, you're Ms. Sophistication. Or at least you look that way. I'm not sure which is really you."

"You noticed that, did you?" She started toward the water, and he followed along the narrow path through the dunes. She sounded relaxed, all the tension that had been between them earlier wiped away. "That's an easy one to explain."

"So go ahead, explain." They reached the hard-packed sand where the walking was easier, and he fell into step with her.

"When I'm here, I revert to the kid I used to be here, growing up. All the cousins do. Just watch sometime when we're doing a crab boil on the beach." She made it sound as if it was a given, that he'd be here to share that. "The boys act like they're about ten, and the girls…well, maybe a year or two older."

"That fits in with something Adam said about the Bodine boys landing on anyone who caused trouble for any one of you."

She glanced up at him. Out here in the moonlight he could see her face better, or maybe his eyes were just growing accustomed to the dark. Right now, her expression was questioning.

"The Bodine boys were terrors, there's no doubt about that. But how did Adam come to say that to you?"

"It was when we were at the docks." How would she react? "He implied that you were protected. I figured he was warning me off."

If he could see colors in the dim light, he'd probably find that she was blushing.

"That nitwit. He shouldn't have said anything of the kind. He certainly ought to have outgrown that kind of nonsense."

She didn't seem to be reading anything into the comment except the surface meaning, and maybe that's all there was.

"So did they really beat up guys who bothered you girls?"

"I don't think it ever went that far." She paused, seeming to examine the tracks of some tiny creature in the glistening wet sand. "There was one kid who came close. He stood me up for my senior prom."

"Sounds like he deserved some grief for that." He was surprised to discover his fists clenching in response to that years-old insult.

"It wasn't as bad as it sounds." She looked up

at him, as if to reinforce the point. "Really. I mean, he was just a guy friend. He never even thought of me romantically. I was just a buddy." She gave an exaggerated sigh, as if laughing at herself. "That was the story of my high school career. I was every guy's best buddy, the one they asked for advice on their girlfriends."

"That doesn't excuse him for dumping you after he'd asked you."

She looked a little disconcerted at his persistence. "It wasn't a big deal, except of course I'd gotten the dress and all. You see, his girl had broken up with him. He told me all about it, and then he asked me to go. But they made up at the last minute, so naturally he wanted to take her."

Naturally. The guy really had deserved pounding. From his limited experience with girls and proms, he'd guess it had been a very big deal indeed.

"So you missed your senior prom." He pictured her crying her eyes out in her crushed gown.

"Goodness, no. Oh, I spent about a half hour moping and crying. Wailing that I loved him. Miz Callie said that if I loved him, I'd want him to have his heart's desire, even if that wasn't me." A smiled touched her lips. "Which pretty much convinced me I hadn't loved him. And Daddy lined up all the Bodine boys who were old enough and told me to take my pick for a prom date."

That was a diverting thought. "Who did you pick?"

"Adam. He was the big football hero. Not that my big brothers weren't impressive, but going with a brother would really have been humiliating. I figured a cousin would be bad enough, but all the girls actually envied me. He was considered quite a catch, believe it or not." She shook her head. "He'll never let me forget that he took me to my senior prom. But it taught me one thing."

"What's that?" Hopefully not to date jerks anymore.

"That August I was off to Columbia for college, and I decided to make myself over. No more being the spunky kid sister and listening to the boys' troubles. I turned myself into the datable girl, not the best buddy girl, and I had fun doing it, too."

The odd thing was that she really thought she'd changed. Oh, she might have altered the exterior, but she was still the good friend everyone relied on, whether she realized it or not.

"I'm still thinking about that idiot who gave up a prom date with you. Didn't he know what he was missing?"

"Missing?" She sounded disconcerted. They'd

come to a stop and stood very close on the shining sand. The breeze off the water ruffled Amanda's hair, blowing strands of silk across her face.

He reached out to slip his fingers into the strands, smoothing them back from her face, letting his palm linger against her cheek. Her eyes widened, and her face tilted toward his in what seemed an involuntary movement.

"He missed this." His voice had roughened, but he couldn't help that. Every cell in his body seemed independently aware of her. "He could have stood on the beach like this with you, touching you. He could have drawn you close." He suited the action to the words, bringing her into the circle of his arms.

She tilted her face back, her hair swinging in a shimmering arc. "I'm glad he didn't," she murmured.

"I'm glad, too." He ran his fingers back through her hair, holding her, caressing the nape of her neck, running his thumb along the smooth line of her chin. "I wouldn't want to be jealous that he'd kissed you."

One tiny part of his mind shouted that this was a mistake, and he shut it up ruthlessly. Mistake or not, they were going to have this moment. He lowered his head, and his lips claimed hers.

Chapter Eleven

Ross's hand clasped Amanda's warmly as they walked back toward the beach house. She might have stayed there locked in his arms forever, but the family would wonder why they were gone so long. Or guess why, more likely.

It didn't matter. Nothing mattered but being here, with him, feeling his hand swallowing up hers while warm waves washed over their bare feet and then receded, shifting the sand restlessly under them.

She should be cautious. Just because she'd tumbled headlong into love didn't mean that he felt the same. But she couldn't stop her feelings, any more than she could stop the ebbing tide.

She glanced up at his face, lit by the moonlight, and smiled.

"What's so funny?" His voice was a low rumble that echoed the sound of the surf.

"You, walking in the water with your pant legs rolled up and your shoes in your hand. A bit different from your usual persona."

His face eased into a returning smile. "It's nice." He sounded surprised.

"Didn't you go to the beach for vacations when you were a child?"

"I suppose, but that was a long time ago. I haven't taken a vacation in—" He stopped, obviously searching his memory. "Not since college, unless you count being unemployed for a time."

"You're overdue for a little relaxation time, then." She'd known he was a workaholic, but that was ridiculous. Everyone needed downtime in order to stay sane.

"I guess I am. You were lucky to grow up in a place like this. With a family like yours."

Only the fact that she was hypersensitive to his speech made her aware of some tension in those last words. Not surprising. The little he'd told her about his parents had made them sound as warm and caring a pair of boa constrictors. She sought for something that would encourage him to open up.

"Miz Callie has always held us all together,

even when we were kids running wild on this beach. Tell me more about your grandmother."

He was silent for a moment. The wavelets washed over their feet, then sucked away toward the ocean again, drawn by its irresistible force.

"She was like your Miz Callie, I suppose. The kind of person who radiates caring. Knowing she loved me gave a center to my life when I was a kid. Whatever conscience and values I have came from her."

"She was a person of faith, then."

He nodded. "She hauled me along to Sunday school and church every Sunday, no excuses. Even after she was gone, I still felt guilty if I tried to sleep in on Sunday mornings."

"And now?" She held her breath, wondering if she was going too far.

He shrugged. "Now I guess I don't know. Somehow God doesn't seem to have much to do with my life."

Her heart clenched. "Miz Callie would say that God has everything to do with it, even if you don't believe."

They'd reached the bottom of the stairs leading up to the deck. Ross stopped, turning her to face him, his hands on her shoulders. "Is that what you'd say, too?"

She nodded. "Yes. I tried the 'sleeping in on Sunday mornings' when I went off to college. It never worked for long. I started feeling like a boat without a rudder when I ignored my faith."

His hands massaged her shoulders gently, and his touch seemed to go right to her heart. "You're pretty special, you know that?"

"Not me." She tried to deny the way her heart fluttered at his words. "Charleston is filled with women like me."

"Then why am I not compelled to kiss any of them?" His lips found hers, and he murmured her name against her mouth.

She wanted to stop thinking entirely, to give herself up to the sensation of being held and cherished in his arms. Of feeling a part of him. But she couldn't quite do that. What he'd revealed about his lack of faith troubled her, and she had to be careful.

He drew back finally, still holding her in the circle of his arms, but looking at her with a faintly troubled expression.

"What's wrong?" she murmured.

"You tell me. It seemed to me you're pulling away."

She wasn't sure what to say. "I guess maybe I don't want to move too fast."

"Maybe you're right." He touched her cheek. "I am still your boss. I wish…"

The sliding glass door above them opened, and footsteps sounded on the deck. "I don't see them," Georgia said. "They must have walked pretty far."

She must be looking down the empty beach, wondering where they'd disappeared to.

"We're here," she called, resigning herself to never knowing what Ross might have said if they hadn't been interrupted. "We'll be right up."

Georgia leaned over the railing to look down at them. "Sorry. I just couldn't wait." Her voice lifted on the words. "We found something."

She vanished again, and Amanda heard her say something to the others. It looked as though the romantic moments were over for now, but that was probably for the best.

Ross touched her shoulder. "We'd better go up before your cousin comes after me."

She started up the stairs, her thoughts returning to that odd exchange he'd mentioned with Adam. What had prompted that?

They walked back into the dining room to find Miz Callie looking slightly dazed. "We might have found him, Amanda. At least, we've found two enlistees who fit. Surely, once we look into them more closely, we'll know. One of them must be Ned."

"Miz Callie, that's wonderful." She bent to hug her grandmother, glancing from face to face.

Georgia was elated, hugging a smiling Matt. Win and Hugh looked pleased. Adam…

Adam didn't seem to be paying any attention to their find. Instead, he was staring at Ross with a look that sent a chill right down her spine.

Cyrus drifted into Ross's office the day after the dinner at Miz Callie's with such a casual look that it was immediately obvious to Ross that something was on his mind. For once, he didn't beat around the bush.

"Where do we stand with the kickback story? Anything happening?" He leaned against the corner of Ross's desk, running one hand over his bushy white hair in a futile attempt to tame it.

Ross lifted his hands, palms up. "Nothing. That's how much I've come up with. Rumors, yes. Hints, odd looks. Facts, no."

"You're not giving up." Cyrus straightened, offended at the thought.

"Of course not." Frustration put an edge to his voice. "As long as there's a thread, I'll keep trying to unravel it. Sometimes that's all it takes—one loose end. I have a lead on somebody who works for a guy who's gotten a suspiciously high number of contracts from the base."

Cyrus grunted approval. "If there's cheating going on, it's our job to expose it. And if we're first to break the story…" He let that trail off, but there was no doubt of the passion he felt. Much as Cyrus claimed to like his gadfly role, he'd give a lot to break this story.

"We'll do our best."

That was all he could promise, and his stomach tightened at the thought that it might not be enough. Maybe he didn't have what it took. Maybe, in this alien place, he'd never be able to come up with the contacts that had fallen so easily into his hands in Washington.

"You'll do it," Cyrus said. "I take it there's nothing to tie Bodine into the scam?"

"Nothing but his position." And Ross's gut instinct telling him that the man didn't like him. But there could be plenty of reasons for that—the main one sitting out in the newsroom right now.

"It'll happen. Look at the story you've nailed starting from a simple complaint from an intern about her air-conditioning."

"That did come together." He couldn't help the satisfaction in his voice. "Jim's writing a sidebar on low-income housing in the city to round it out, and we break it in tomorrow's paper."

Cyrus's eyes glinted, and he rubbed his palms together. "That'll show 'em. I read Amanda's piece, by the way. She did a great job with that interview. Heart-tugging without being maudlin, presented the people with dignity. There's more to that young woman than I thought, and I'll be the first to admit it. I was judging her on her appearance, and there's substance there."

"It wasn't bad." The lukewarm words hid a rush of pleasure at hearing Amanda praised. She had really risen to the challenge he'd thrown at her.

"Guess it's time to give her somethin' substantial to work on." Cyrus's bushy brows drew down. "Unless we have to expose her daddy for a thief. I reckon we'll see her back mighty fast if that happens."

When Cyrus started sounding folksy, that meant that he was worried.

Well, Cyrus had company in that. Ross had let himself get involved with Amanda, despite all the good reasons not to. If this situation turned sour, a lot of people were going to get hurt.

He seemed to see Amanda's face, turned up to his in the moonlight, and his heart clenched. If that happened, how was he going to live with himself?

Amanda dragged her mind back to the words on her computer screen. It was something of a comedown to go from the excitement of breaking the slumlord story to writing an article about the barbecue cook-off for charity the *Bugle* was sponsoring on the weekend. Too bad every story couldn't involve controversy.

Still, it made her understand a bit about Ross's attitude toward his profession. And why he felt his real life was back in D.C., where he could go from one important story to another.

He'll go back to that, a small voice whispered in the back of her mind. *He'll go back, eventually. And then where will you be?* And even if he didn't, were they really suited to each other? Each time they got close, it seemed she saw something in his values to push her away.

"Amanda."

She looked up, startled, to find her cousin Adam standing in front of her desk. By the patient look on his face, he must have been standing there for a bit.

"Adam, sorry. The receptionist didn't let me know you're here."

"She knows me by now. That must be some important story you're working on to take you that far away."

"Just daydreaming," she said quickly. She waved toward a chair. "Have a seat. What's up?"

He sat down, reaching over to drop a manila envelope on the desk. "Truth is that I need your opinion on something." He tapped the envelope with one finger. "I've been doing some research, trying to find something that will tell us which one of our possible candidates is Uncle Ned."

"If either," Amanda said. "I know Miz Callie is convinced we're almost there, but…"

"I know, I know. That's why I want you to look at this. Be sure it's not just wishful thinking on my part before I take it to Miz Callie."

"What?" She reached for the envelope, but before she could take it, Adam emptied its contents onto her desk. A black-and-white photo slid out, as well as a magnifying glass.

"Take a look." He put the photo in front of her. "You'll need the magnifier to make out the faces. Tell me if you see anyone familiar."

Amanda pressed the edges of the photo flat. It was a copy, she'd guess, of an old picture. Adam, with his latest photo software, would probably have sharpened it as much as possible.

The black-and-white photo showed a PT boat docked someplace where there was sandy beach and palm trees in the background. The boat's crew posed for the camera, grinning self-consciously.

Her heart clenched at those young faces, staring out at her from more than a half century ago. They were filled with so much bravado.

"That was taken when she'd just arrived in the war zone," Adam said. "She had a full complement then, not tested in battle yet." He spoke of the PT boat with as much familiarity as he'd talk of his own patrol boat. "See if you recognize anyone."

Obediently she took the magnifier. Were they going to find out what had happened to Ned Bodine at last? Her pulse beat rapidly, and she paused a moment to steady herself before bending over the image.

Take it slow, study each face methodically. Adam trusted her to do this right and not send Miz Callie off on a wild-goose chase.

She worked from the right to the left, focusing on each face, searching for any trace of familiarity. Nothing. Then she moved the glass to the group on the left.

The face jumped out at her, so clear that she

couldn't help a gasp. She planted her finger on the figure. "There. That's Ned. It has to be."

"You sure, sugar? The features are pretty washed-out on an old photo like this."

"It's not just the features." She struggled to explain the sense of familiarity that gripped her. "It's not just the features, although they're right, what you can see of them. It's the way he holds himself, the way his hand rests on the boat's hull, like he's caressing it." She grinned, sure of herself. "I've seen you do the same, more times than I can count."

Adam's face relaxed. "I see something of our Win in him, myself. That tilt of the head, maybe."

Funny how gestures and movements could pass through generations as surely as coloring. "Which one of the two names Miz Callie picked out is he?"

"Theodore Hawkins." He didn't need to explain that Hawkins was the name of Granddad's mother's family. "I guess he wanted to take something of family with him."

"I guess he did." She touched the photograph lightly. "Do you know what happened to him?"

"Not yet, but it shouldn't take long now that we have a name. One thing I do know." His face sobered. "The PT boat went down in the South China Sea in '44."

Her eyes filled with tears, and she brushed them away impatiently. "Well, we thought from the beginning that he probably didn't survive the war, since the family never heard from him. Miz Callie will be relieved to know the truth."

He nodded, standing and scooping the photo and magnifier back into the envelope. "I'm gonna run over there a bit later to show her what we have. It'll take a couple days, probably, to get the complete military records. You want to come with me?"

"I can't, not tonight." She glanced at her watch. "I'm meeting someone for dinner. You go, and take all the credit. You deserve it."

That didn't bring the smile she expected. "This date—it wouldn't be with Ross Lockhart, would it?"

"Yes, why?" She sat up straighter, prepared to do battle. Adam's attitude toward Ross was just ridiculous, and she didn't mind telling him so.

"Look, sugar, don't fly off the handle with me." He obviously had no trouble interpreting her mood. "I just… I don't want you to get hurt. I don't trust him."

She blew out an exasperated breath. "For pity's

sake, Adam. I'm a big girl now. I don't need the Bodine boys to protect me from my dates."

"That's not what I mean." Adam frowned, planting one fist against her desktop. "Maybe he's a nice enough guy in some ways, but I'd say there's not much he'd stick at when it comes to getting a big story."

True, but… "That's what makes him a good reporter."

"Even if he's after a story that involves your family?" The question burst out of him, and then he clamped his mouth shut as if instantly regretting it.

She shot out of her chair, facing him over the width of her desk. "What are you talking about? What could he possibly want to write that would affect us? If you're talking about that business with Ned—well, we've practically got the proof in hand that he wasn't a coward."

Adam dismissed that with a wave of his hand. "His digging is more up-to-date than that. If he—" He stopped, shook his head. "Look, I can't say more."

"Adam." Her voice warned. "You tell me what's going on right this minute."

"I can't." To do him credit, he looked miserable at having brought it up. "Maybe I'm imagining things, but has it occurred to you that this series he's supposed to be doing about the Coast Guard base might be a cover for something else?"

"No." She tried for an indignant tone, but it didn't quite ring true. Daddy's unexplained animosity toward Ross, Ross's insistence on information that didn't seem to have much to do with the supposed purpose of the articles…

"I'm sorry, sugar." His voice went soft. "I don't want to cause trouble. Just—be careful."

Before she could say anything, he turned and walked quickly away.

Chapter Twelve

Amanda was still troubled by Adam's words when she stepped through the front door of the Shem Creek Café that evening. She shook the rain from her umbrella and shoved it into the old-fashioned milk can that held a number of similarly wet umbrellas. The storm that was making its way up the coast promised them a couple of inches of much-needed rain before all was said and done.

The rain hadn't kept folks away from the popular restaurant, and the tables and booths were already crowded. As the hostess moved toward her, she scanned the dining area and spotted Ross, half rising to catch her eye from a table next to the window.

"That's okay, I see my..." What? Date? Boyfriend? She wasn't sure either of those words applied to her tenuous relationship with Ross.

Fortunately, the waitress didn't bother to wait for her to finish the sentence, waving her into the dining room with a smile.

Amanda wove her way between the tables, trying to suppress the flutter that arose somewhere in her mid-section when she saw Ross waiting for her, his eyes warming as he watched her.

Ridiculously aware of his gaze on her, she nearly stumbled into a tray rack that had been left between the tables to trip up the distracted. *Get hold of yourself,* she lectured. *This isn't just about being with Ross tonight. You have to find out if what Adam hinted at is true.*

If she didn't, the suspicion would poison whatever relationship she and Ross had. She couldn't pretend the feeling wasn't there. She had to deal with it.

Adam's words had crystallized the amorphous concern that had been drifting like fog in the back of her thoughts. She'd realized after he left that she'd already been wondering why she'd never seen any indication that Ross had written a word about the interviews she'd set up.

Certainly he'd been researching something. Jim had commented on that, saying he'd surprised Ross searching through some records late in the evening, when he'd thought the offices deserted. And Ross never had asked to see any of the photos she'd taken, or checked with her on anything to do with the Coast Guard.

"Amanda." He said her name with a caressing note that he'd never use in the office. "I'm glad you're here."

"I hope I didn't keep you waiting long." She slid into the chair he pulled out for her, too aware of the treacherous effect his nearness had on her as he bent to push the chair in. She could only hope the anxiety she felt wasn't written on her face.

Anxiety—that was probably the right word. The truth was that she'd rather not face this. She'd rather pretend everything was fine and enjoy the moment.

"I've just been here a few minutes," he said. "Cyrus advised me to come early so I could get a table at the window to enjoy the view."

"Cyrus knows we're out tonight together?" She wasn't sure she liked that thought.

"Cyrus knows everything. Sometimes I wonder if he doesn't have a closed-circuit television watching our every move."

"Not here, I hope." She glanced around with a mock shudder.

"Just at work." His face relaxed in a smile.

Her heart clutched. She hadn't ever seen quite that much ease in his expression. Even when he'd been enjoying himself as he had, she felt sure, with Miz Callie, there'd been a hint of restraint, of things suppressed and guarded.

This was the way he could be, if he weren't so eaten up with the wrongs that had been dealt him.

Please, Father. The prayer formed almost without volition. *Please help him set himself free from all that holds him back from being an open, giving person.*

"Have you had a look at the menu?" She'd been silent too long, caught up in her reactions to him. "I highly recommend the she-crab soup. And the shrimp and grits."

"Do they guarantee that only she-crabs went into the soup?" The teasing note in his voice turned her determination to jelly.

"I'm sure they do. Anyway, it's the best I've ever eaten."

"Okay, then. She-crab soup and a grilled sirloin."

She raised her eyebrows at that. "You did notice that saltwater tank when we came in, didn't you? Why would you order steak in a place that has seafood only a step from the boats?"

She nodded to the window beside them. A lone

fishing boat made its way up the creek, its captain swathed in a yellow slicker against the rain.

"You're not going to let me get away with this, are you?" He flipped the menu open again. "I'm not ready to try shrimp and grits yet. Will you be satisfied if I get the grouper?"

"I guess. But sometime you have to give in and try grits."

They could go on all evening like this, as far as she was concerned. Keep the tone light and easy, enjoy the moment. Not think about the questions she had to ask.

"Maybe I can have a bite of yours," he said softly, reaching across the table to touch her fingertips with his in a gesture that set her pulse fluttering.

The server came then, and after a consultation as to what the catch of the day was, she brought drinks and headed back to the kitchen with their order.

"This is in the nature of a celebration," Ross said, tipping his glass of iced tea toward hers.

"It is?"

He nodded. "We've put the story to bed. In the morning it will be all over the city. Cyrus was very complimentary about your writing, by the way."

Cyrus was? "I'll have to thank him," she said.

"All right." His fingers enveloped hers. "Your

piece was better than good. You're not quite the lightweight I thought you were at first."

"At first? You've had me pegged as the stereotypical Southern belle right along, and I'm not sure you're over it yet."

"Maybe so," he admitted. "You have to admit, you do look and sound the part."

"Scarlett O'Hara has a lot to answer for," she said darkly. "And let me tell you, Scarlett was a lot tougher than she looked."

"Got it," he said, lifting one hand in a gesture of surrender. "I promise not to make that mistake again. I couldn't, not now that I know you." His voice deepened on the words, and his eyes seemed to darken.

Her breath caught in her throat. She couldn't have given him a flippant answer if her life depended on it. Adam's worry sounded in her mind, adding its weight to the doubts she couldn't get rid of.

Their food arrived then, and she was grateful for the distraction. They ate, they sampled each other's entrées, and then Ross pinned her with a direct gaze.

"I saw you and Adam in the newsroom today. It looked like a pretty serious discussion."

She smoothed her napkin out in her lap. It

seemed she was being forced to have this talk no matter how she tried to avoid it.

"He brought a photo over to show me." She was still avoiding, and she knew it. "He's been trying to identify which of our possibilities is the right one, and he found an old picture of the crew of a PT boat that Theodore Hawkins served on. It was Uncle Ned. I'm sure of it." Her eyes filled with tears at the memory of that young face. "The family will be so relieved to know the truth about him at last."

"After all these years," he said, shaking his head a little. "There's a human interest story there, if you're not too close to write it."

"I hadn't thought of that."

Her nerve endings prickled. She hadn't, but that could be the resolution to all their worries about Miz Callie and the memorial to Ned Bodine. If the world, meaning Charleston in this case, learned first that Ned hadn't been a coward, but had served honorably, then no one could argue about Miz Callie establishing a memorial to him.

"Is that everything?"

She looked up, meeting his gaze, to find a question in his eyes.

"I…I don't know what you mean." She certainly was feeble as a liar.

"Yes, you do. Something's been weighing on you." His dark brows furrowed, setting three vertical lines between them. "Was Adam warning you against me again?"

"Not the way you mean." She couldn't leave it at that. Despair settled on her. What she said next was going to send Ross back behind his armor. She'd prayed that he'd be set free, but accusing him wouldn't do that, would it?

"What then?" His tone turned impatient.

She took a breath. There was no way out but to say it. "Are you really writing a series of human interest articles about the Coast Guard base? Or is it a cover for something else going on?"

She watched it happen. His face tightened into a mask. His eyes grew cold and suspicious.

"What makes you think that?"

They were both answering questions with questions. That didn't get them anywhere.

"I don't just think it. I feel it. There was something going on when you talked with my father. You went in there with an agenda, and it didn't have anything to do with writing a profile piece."

She waited for the ax to fall, knowing she'd said nothing more than the truth.

"People who haven't done anything wrong don't have to worry about publicity," he said finally. "That's all I have to say about it, so you might pass that on to your cousin. And the form these articles take is my business and Cyrus's."

Not yours. The words were unspoken, but there.

All the barricades had gone up between them again. And any chance she had of finding out who Ross truly was at heart had just moved further away.

Amanda tried to put aside her worries and enjoy the air of celebration that permeated the newsroom the next day. The slumlord exposé had been everything Cyrus might have wished for—a splashy story of wide interest, a clear villain and, best of all, the *Bugle* had beaten out the competition.

The television in the corner of the newsroom was turned on, with local stations belatedly jumping on the bandwagon, promising exciting new revelations about Hardy on the noon news.

A grumble greeted this, but Cyrus, watching with the others, turned away with a shrug. "That's their advantage, going on the air right away. People are still going to come to us if they want something more than a couple minutes' worth of sound bites."

"Right." Even Jim, whom no one could

remember seeing smile since a certain prominent local politician had been caught trying to pick up an undercover policewoman, had a broad grin on his face. "We do our job, they do theirs. Good work, everyone."

Most of the staff had had little or nothing to do with the story, but its success affected them, too. Amanda suspected that the old warhorses, like Jim, were reminded of what it had been like in their glory days, while the eager kids saw their dreams of journalism coming true.

The buzz died off suddenly. If it was Ross…her stomach lurched. They'd parted with an uncomfortable truce last night, and she couldn't imagine that there would be any more romantic dinners on their horizon for a while, at least.

But it was C.J. who'd come in. She paused, looking around rather truculently, as if prepared for a fight.

Jim walked over and threw an arm over her shoulder in a hug that would have staggered Amanda, but didn't seem to faze C.J. "Good work on that story, kid. You led us to a really fine piece. We couldn't have done it without you."

Following Jim's lead, the others in the newsroom added their congratulations. By the time C.J. made it to Amanda's desk, she wore a broad grin.

She dropped into the chair beside the desk, a little doubt creeping into her eyes. "D'you think they really mean it? I didn't do much. If it wasn't for my gran, I'd never have talked to you about it."

"They mean it," Amanda assured her. "Even if you had second thoughts, your instincts were right on target."

"That's right." Ross's deep voice startled her, even as it reverberated right down to her bones. How did he manage to get within a few feet without her knowing he was coming? "Instincts are a solid part of being a good reporter. You can learn how to construct a story, but you can't learn instinct."

C.J. ducked her head, embarrassed at being singled out by the managing editor.

"Trust your instincts," he said, this time looking right at Amanda.

She lifted her chin. "Sometimes your instincts can tear you in two directions at the same time." Between the man you cared about and your family, for instance.

"If you're in doubt, go with the truth." He'd given up any pretense that he was talking to C.J., his gray eyes focused laserlike on Amanda's face. "That's the only thing reporters have going for them in the long run."

"And if you're not sure what the truth is?"

"Then you'd better find out, if you're any kind of a reporter." He spun and stalked off.

"You want to tell me what that was all about?" C.J. was probably too astonished to be tactful, if she ever was anyway.

"Nothing." She took a breath and shook her head. "Well, nothing I can talk about. How are things between your grandmother and the other people in your building?"

C.J. shrugged, seeming to accept the new subject. "The other folks are all over the place. Some of them are complaining about the news crews out front, and some are offering them guided tours and acting like they broke the story themselves. Some of them are blaming us for bringing all this fuss on them. And I guess some are just plain scared."

"How's your grandmother taking it?" That was exactly the thing they had feared would happen to Miz Callie if she went through with her plans—that people she cared about would turn against her.

"She just holds her head high and ignores them." C.J. gave a little shrug that probably expressed bafflement. "I want to punch someone. Not sure I'll ever get to where she is."

"Give yourself some time." That was probably good advice for her, too, when she wondered if she'd ever be the woman her grandmother was. "And don't forget about calling the attorney if there's anything you don't understand. He's there to help you."

"I won't forget. And no chance I'll forget what you did."

"What I did? It was you and your grandmother who did it. And Mr. Lockhart, of course, who started the investigation."

"I didn't mean that." C.J. lowered her gaze in embarrassment. "I mean what you said that day at the Market. About having courage. It seems like that really affected my gran. She's got her nerve back in a big way, ready to conquer the world. Says I'm going to college if she has to bully me all the way. She'll do it, too."

"I don't doubt it." She smiled, thinking how alike C.J.'s grandmother and Miz Callie were under the skin. Miz Callie would do that, too, if she thought one of her grandkids needed it.

"She sent this for you." C.J. put a paper bag in Amanda's hands. "She said don't you give me no arguments about takin' it, either."

Even without unwrapping it, Amanda knew by the touch what it was. A sweetgrass basket. She opened the bag and pulled it out, her breath catching.

Not just a sweetgrass basket, a work of art. It was an egg basket, the delicate oval shape complemented by striations, layering dark against light in an endless spiral.

"It's beautiful." She knew better than to try to return it. That would be an insult to the woman and to C.J. "I don't know how to thank her. I'll cherish this."

"I guess that's all the thanks she'd want." C.J.'s eyes were suspiciously bright. "She said to tell you something else. She said to remind you that strong women have the courage to do what's right."

Amanda turned the words over in her mind as she turned the basket over in her hands. C.J.'s grandmother had echoed her own words back at her, with a twist. Was she that kind of strong woman? She wasn't sure, but it was time she started acting as if she was.

Chapter Thirteen

The rain had stopped by the time Amanda arrived on Isle of Palms that afternoon to cover the festival the newspaper was cosponsoring to benefit the elementary school that served the two barrier islands. Cyrus's philanthropy could be erratic. It was hard to tell what worthy cause would catch his fancy, but he regularly used the newspaper to sponsor events that needed a bit of help.

She moved among the crowds along Front Street, past the Windjammer Café and rows of shops. The street was lined with booths of all sorts, many of them featuring local delicacies or handcrafted items. Beyond the buildings, the dunes ran down to the sea, gray and angry-looking today. Somewhere out there the slow-moving tropical storm had stalled, a situation that made coastal dwellers edgy.

She had more than the weather or the festival in mind at the moment, though. Daddy was off duty today, she'd learned by a phone call to her mother. He'd announced his plan to stop by the festival, even though Mamma couldn't come because it was her day to volunteer at the hospital; everybody knew that, and she couldn't possibly disappoint folks who were counting on her.

Assuring her mother that she understood, Amanda had gotten off the phone. Mamma didn't know why it was so important to Amanda to catch up to Daddy today, and Amanda surely didn't plan to tell her.

She had to confront Daddy and find out what was going on between him and Ross. She hadn't had much success with Ross, but she certainly could manage her own father better than that.

And there he was. Not giving her nerves a chance to fail, Amanda hurried her steps, catching up with him in front of a fishing game booth, where small children were dipping with their nets in pursuit of colorful plastic fish.

"You plannin' on going fishing, Daddy?" She slid her arm in his.

He jerked around, nearly throwing her off balance. "Manda. What on earth are you doing here?"

Keeping her smile fixed with an effort, she gestured to the camera slung around her neck. "I'm covering the event for the newspaper. Didn't you know we were a cosponsor?"

What was going on with Daddy? He'd jerked around like a…like a criminal, feeling the hand of the law on his shoulder. She shoved the thought away.

"No, no, can't say I did." He sounded distracted. "I just figured one of us ought to come and support the school, and your mamma was tied up at the hospital today." He loosened her grip on his arm. "Well, I'll let you get on with your work. I'm fixin' to pick up a shrimp burger for my lunch and see if I can find some little somethin' to take to your mamma."

She caught his arm again. "Not so fast, Daddy. I need to talk to you."

"If you're working—" he began, but she cut him off.

"Daddy, I have to know. What's going on between you and Ross Lockhart?"

There was the faintest hesitation, and then he

was shaking his head. "I don't know what you're talking about, child."

"You know exactly what I'm talking about." She wanted to shake him. "For goodness' sake, I even had Adam coming by the office to tell me to stay away from the man because of it, whatever it is."

Daddy scowled, his square face flushing. "Adam ought to know enough to hold his tongue."

"Adam is worried about me. I think he's afraid I'm going to get squashed like a bug between the two of you. And I'm worried about you." There, it was a relief to say the words. "Everyone's stumbling around in the dark. Just tell me."

Her father's color deepened. "You ought to know that there's some things I can't talk to you about, Amanda. Can't even talk to your mamma, for that matter, and I tell her everything."

She felt it slipping away from her, and she tried to hang on with both hands. "Ross Lockhart is my boss. That means I'm involved, whether I want to be or not. Why does Adam think I need protecting? Why did you and Ross act like you were old enemies the first time you met? What were you hiding from him?"

"Hush up." Daddy darted a quick look around, but no one was close enough to hear their low voices. "I can't talk about it, Amanda. If you want to know something about your boss, you'd better ask him."

"I have." She met his gaze steadily. *Oh, Daddy. I trust you. Just don't shut me out.*

Daddy's face tightened. "What did he say?"

"He said the innocent don't need to worry about publicity."

She expected him to explode at that. Expected, but didn't get it. Instead, her father seemed to be looking at someone or something over her shoulder. His muscles had gone tight, and his expression actually scared her.

"I can't talk anymore right now." He gave her a little shove. "Take yourself and your cameras off, and forget I'm here."

"Daddy—"

"I mean it, Amanda." It was his tone of command, the one she'd never disobeyed in her life. "I'll talk to you later. Right now, just go."

There was no arguing with that. She turned, tears blurring her eyes. What on earth was her father mixed up in?

Ross ducked behind an ice cream stand when Amanda turned to look in his direction. If she saw him, she'd think he didn't trust her to cover the event.

The truth was far from that, but he didn't intend to enlighten her. He'd had another tip, and this time he'd realized that the informant had to work for Cliff Winchell, the contractor who'd been so evasive each time Ross had called.

He couldn't make too much of that fact. Plenty of innocent people didn't want to talk to the press. But Winchell was also the man whose company seemed to get more than its share of contracts from the Coast Guard base.

According to the informant, Winchell was meeting today at the festival with his contact from the base. And sure enough, there the man was, working his way from booth to booth as if he had nothing better to do with himself today but buy a candy apple.

Ross stationed himself by the ice cream stand, to the annoyance of the vendor, and casually watched the man. Still, he couldn't keep himself from glancing at Amanda from time to time.

She moved, and he was able to see who she was talking to. His stomach jolted. Amanda turned, walking away from her father, the distress on her face plain even from this distance.

Her pain caught at his heart, turning it cold. He should never have let things go as far as they had between them. She was going to be hurt—was already hurting, and he'd probably make it worse before he was done.

But how could he have resisted her? He'd come from a situation where everyone he knew and trusted had turned against him. Even the rescue Cyrus offered had been conditional.

But Amanda—there was nothing conditional about Amanda. Interest in everyone whose life she touched poured from her like a welcome stream in the desert. She had a good heart. His grandmother would have said those simple words in the highest of praise.

Winchell started moving oh so casually, along the row of buildings that lined the street. Ross followed, cutting through the crowd at an angle that would keep him well away from Amanda.

He could avoid encountering her, but he couldn't dismiss her from his mind that easily. That talk they'd had about faith—he hadn't been able to stop the flow of memories that had loosened.

He'd drifted far from the faith to which his grandmother had led him, maybe too far to go back. After her death, he'd gone along with the people who were his friends at school—high achievers who focused on success and achievement. Faith seemed to have little to do with that.

Winchell was walking along the sidewalk, stopping to stare at a restaurant menu posted in a window. Looking at that, or using the plate glass to see if he was being followed? Ross kept back, well out of range of the glass.

Amanda had admitted drifting, too, when she went away to school. Probably a lot of people did. But she'd come back to the faith of her childhood. Back to the center of her life, she'd implied.

He didn't have that. Maybe she didn't, either, his cynical mind retorted. Maybe she just thought she did, under the influence of the family she loved. How could she know?

Winchell, apparently satisfied no one was watching him, slipped between the buildings and disappeared. Ross elbowed his way through a group of teenagers blocking the sidewalk and narrowly escaped being hit by the swinging camera of a sunburned tourist.

He reached the place where the man vanished. A narrow passageway ran between the buildings. At the end of it, he could glimpse dunes and sea oats. Nothing else, but Winchell had gone this way, so he would, too.

When he neared the end of the passageway, he slowed, moving cautiously, and peered around the corner. There was his quarry, perhaps twenty yards away in the dunes, gesticulating wildly, facing another man. Amanda's father.

Oddly, there was no satisfaction at seeing a difficult case come together. Just sorrow and anger at what the man was inflicting on his family. On Amanda. Brett Bodine would hurt so many innocent people with his duplicity.

Pain had a grip on his throat, but he pulled the small camera from his pocket. This time he wouldn't be caught by faked photos. He'd provide the proof himself, and no one would be able to question it.

If she concentrated hard enough on her job, Amanda decided, she just might be able to ignore that unsatisfying conversation with her father. Or pretend to.

She'd interviewed one of the organizers of the event and picked up a quote from a teacher at the school. A few grinning students had been happy to have their picture taken. They'd been enjoying the festival as much for the fun it provided on an uncharacteristically gray July day as for the money it would raise for their school.

Still, that was okay. It was their engaging grins she'd been after.

What else might Cyrus think was important to

her report? Since he was a sponsor, he'd cast a particularly critical eye on whatever she brought in. It was a wonder he wasn't here in person, supervising.

She rounded the corner of a white-elephant stand, run by the ladies of one of the island's churches, and spotted the one person she definitely hadn't expected to see here. Ross.

He hadn't noticed her yet. She could slip back around the stand and avoid another awkward conversation.

Then she noticed the camera he carried, and annoyance swept away any other consideration. She walked up to him with quick strides. As if he sensed her approach, he swung around to face her.

"Amanda." He looked almost startled to see her, as if he didn't remember sending her.

"Amanda," she agreed. "The person you sent to cover this event." Disappointment that he so obviously still didn't have confidence in her lent an edge to her voice. "What's wrong? Didn't you trust me to do this? You even brought your own camera."

He seemed to give himself a mental shake, and he slid the camera into his pocket. "Don't be ridiculous." His tone was just as sharp as hers had been. "If I didn't think you could handle the assignment, I assure you, you wouldn't be here."

That she almost believed. When it came to work, Ross didn't know the meaning of the word *tact*.

"I see. Then do you mind my asking why you're here, too?"

He shrugged, glancing away from her as if fascinated by the daily specials chalked on a board in front of the nearest restaurant. "Cyrus thought a representative from the paper should be here all day. He's tied up in a meeting at the moment, so I'm his deputy."

It was perfectly plausible, knowing Cyrus. She'd buy the story if she didn't know him so well. He wasn't meeting her eyes.

"Have you met with the organizers yet?" she asked, sure she knew the answer.

"Not yet. I'll do it." He gave her a baffled, irritated look. "If you have what you came for, you can head on back to the office."

"It sounds as if you want to be rid of me. What's going on?"

"Nothing except that I don't want you to waste any more of the *Bugle*'s time."

She almost wished she couldn't read him so easily. This connection between them was going to be difficult enough to end without that.

She'd come to know him so well in such a short

time—had gone from disliking him to grudging admiration to caring to love. And now it was over.

The angry glance he directed at her didn't bother her, because she could see something else lurking in the depths of his brown eyes. Something that might almost be pity.

Her heart lurched. Why would Ross be looking at her as if he felt sorry for her?

"Amanda."

The curt voice had her spinning to face her father. He looked—frozen. Bleak. And suddenly she couldn't breathe.

"Daddy, what is it?" Who is it? That was the question. Who is hurt, or worse, to make you look that way?

"I need you to go out to the beach house to stay with your grandmother."

She nodded, trying to find the words to ask.

"A fishing boat swamped." He jerked his head toward the gray ocean, seeming to force the words out. "Win went after a survivor. He's missing." He held up his hand to still her questions. "I don't know anything else. I'm headed for the post. I'll call you at the beach house as soon as I have anything."

Anything. Like whether her laughing, loving, daredevil of a cousin was alive or dead.

Daddy drew her close for a quick, hard hug. She resisted the urge to cling to him. He didn't need that now.

"I'll take care of Miz Callie. It's okay. I'll call the others. Just go." Her voice choked, in spite of her effort to keep it level. "I love you, Daddy."

Chapter Fourteen

Amanda wasn't fit to drive after a shock like that. At least, that's what Ross told himself as he took the wheel of her car. He pulled onto Palm Boulevard and turned toward Sullivan's Island. He wasn't all that familiar with the barrier islands, but finding his way around them wasn't hard, since each had only one main street running its length.

He sent a sideways glance toward Amanda. For the first few minutes of the drive she'd huddled in the passenger seat, gaze turned inward, hands clasped in her lap. He realized she was praying.

Then she straightened, pulling the cell phone from her bag, and began calling. The first few calls ended in left messages, it seemed. *Call me, right away.*

Finally she reached someone. Her brother Hugh, it sounded like. After a few emotional exchanges she disconnected and turned to him.

"Hugh knows a little more than what Daddy told me. Not much." She was making an effort to keep her voice steady, he could tell, and his heart twisted.

"What did he say?"

"A fishing boat capsized about thirty miles out. Not a commercial one—a twenty-two-foot private boat, from what he'd been able to find out." She pressed her lips together for an instant. "They shouldn't have been out that far, not in six-to-eight-foot seas. Most likely a wave swamped them, and they were in the water before they even knew what happened."

"How many people were onboard?" He couldn't keep his mind from working like a reporter's, even in these circumstances.

"He didn't know. Two or three, from what he'd heard." Her hands clasped together in her lap, straining until her knuckles were white.

"Win was in the chopper that went out." That much was obvious, so he'd save her from saying it again.

She nodded. "They radioed back that they'd spotted the overturned boat with two survivors clinging to it. One of them didn't have a life jacket. Win insisted on jumping. Hugh said the account got sketchy after that. He didn't know what happened with the chopper, or how Win went missing, or…" Her voice broke.

He covered her hand with his. "Hold on. They should know more soon." He had no idea if that was true, but his heart ached for her and it was the only comforting thing he could think of to say.

"Hugh's on his way to the base. He'll call back as soon as he gets on duty."

"I thought Hugh was a cop." Wasn't that what she'd said when she talked about her brother?

"Coast Guard. Maritime law enforcement," she said briefly.

Of course. He would be. And what would Hugh think if his uncle was exposed as a crook?

They crossed the bridge between the islands at Breech Inlet, and he glanced out at the gray, angry-looking ocean under an equally gray sky. How long could someone survive in that? Win was in good shape, but even so…

"I'm surprised they let Win jump when it's this bad out."

She looked surprised. "That's what he does. 'I'm a Coast Guard rescue swimmer. I'm here to help you.' That's what they say when they go after someone. The other boys tease him about that." Her voice trembled a bit on the words. She took an audible breath. "But that says it all, really. I know Win can come across as flippant and brash, but underneath, he's solid. *Semper Paratus*. Always Ready."

"I don't doubt that." It was steadying her to talk, it seemed. A good thing, given what she'd have to deal with this day.

She nodded, picking up the phone again. "I'd better try to make a few more calls. Daddy will call Win's folks, but everyone else has to be told." She paused. "Thanks. For driving me. For listening."

"Anytime."

Anytime, he thought as she started calling again. There wouldn't be any other times, probably, to talk or listen or anything else.

The camera weighted his pocket. It was like carrying a loaded grenade. Once those photos hit the paper, the lives of all the Bodines would change immeasurably. And Amanda would never speak to him again.

He couldn't change who he was. He couldn't change the truth.

She was talking to her twin. He recognized the note in her voice that only seemed to be there when she spoke with Annabel.

"Love you," she said, clicking off just as he pulled up at the beach house.

She was out of the car in an instant, and then she stopped, clinging to the car door. He hurried around to her and took her arm.

"Okay?"

Her eyes were dark with hurt. "No one else has gotten here yet. They wouldn't tell Miz Callie on the phone. I'll have to tell her."

"You can do it." His fingers tightened on her arm. "She's a strong woman. She can deal with it."

"You're right." Her eyes focused on his face. "I appreciate—" She stopped, as if suddenly realizing something. "I forgot that you drove my car. You can take it back, if you want. Or I'll call a cab for you—"

"Forget it. I'll stick around, as long as I can be useful."

Her expression went guarded. "Not to write about."

"No. Just to help."

He'd do this, and it was the last thing she'd ever let him do for her.

He followed her up the steps to the beach house, trying to find a little extra armor for what was to come. He couldn't pretend he was very good at dealing with other people's emotions.

Maybe that was why he'd never be able to write the sort of story that Amanda had done about C.J. and her grandmother. He just didn't have that sort of caring in him, apparently.

Amanda opened the unlocked front door, calling out as she did so. "Miz Callie?"

A quick, light step sounded, and Amanda's grandmother emerged from the kitchen, shedding a straw hat and sunglasses as she did so.

"Amanda. Ross. What a nice surprise. I just came in from—" She broke off, looking from one face to the other, and her smile vanished. There was silence for the space of a heartbeat.

"Who?" she asked.

"It's Win, Miz Callie."

Amanda went to put her arm around her grandmother. He moved to her other side, ready to grab her if she started to sag. But Miz Callie, it seemed, was made of sterner stuff than that. She leaned against Amanda for just a second, and then she straightened.

"How bad?"

"He's missing. We don't know much more." Amanda guided her grandmother to the sofa and sat beside her, holding her hands. "He went in after a victim…"

The phone rang. Amanda signaled to him to

answer it. She continued talking to Miz Callie, her voice steady.

Amanda was a strong woman in a family filled with them. Too bad he'd let himself be blind to that for so long.

He took the cordless phone into the kitchen to answer it. "Bodine residence."

"Hugh Bodine here. Who is this?" A male voice barked.

"Ross Lockhart. I drove Amanda over."

"Good. She shouldn't be alone." Hugh, at least, didn't seem to share the family suspicion of him.

"She's talking to your grandmother now. Do you want me to get her?"

"Don't bother. I'll tell you what I've found out, and you can relay it to them." If anything, Hugh sounded relieved to have someone who wasn't emotionally involved take over that chore.

"Amanda's told me what she already knows, so just go from there." *And don't expect me to break the worst news, because I won't.*

"The weather was bad, but I guess you can see that for yourself. Two survivors. The pilot radioed the coordinates, said he was having trouble keeping the helo steady in the wind. Win jumped, we know that."

"What happened to the chopper?"

"Nearly went down, but the pilot managed to pull it out. They limped back to base." Frustration edged Hugh's voice. "Choppers are grounded. You'll have to tell them that, of course, but be sure they know every available craft is out looking."

"I will." Even from a layman's viewpoint, he knew that had to be bad news.

"Give me your cell number," Hugh said abruptly. "That way, I can be sure to get you if…"

He let that trail off, but Ross could fill in the blanks. If he had to relay something bad, Hugh wanted it told in person, not over the phone. Ross reeled off the number, hung up and walked back into the living room, carrying the phone.

Amanda and her grandmother stared at him, their expressions nearly identical. Hope. Fear. Need.

"That was Hugh." Sitting down across from them, he repeated the substance of Hugh's message. "He said to tell you that every available craft is out there. He'll call back the instant he has anything more."

They were silent for a moment. Then Miz Callie held out her hand to him. "Let's pray."

He couldn't refuse, any more than he could have refused his own grandmother, and he hoped his reluctance didn't show on his face. If God was there, Ross couldn't imagine He'd want to hear from him.

Amanda took his other hand, her grip firm, and his pulse accelerated.

"Dear Father," Miz Callie began, sounding as if she talked to a close friend. Her voice was calm and confident as she prayed, asking for God's protection for all those in peril, especially Win and the two people he was trying to save.

The sense that he was a fraud slipped away from Ross as she prayed. He might not have been able to pray himself, but as he listened, he found his heart gradually creaking open to the possibility that not only was God there, but He cared what happened to Win, to the victims, to those who waited and those who struggled to find them.

"Amen," she said softly, and the word felt like a benediction.

Ross opened his eyes, shaking his head a little as if it needed clearing. What had just happened? He didn't want to start wondering, start questioning. He wasn't looking for God.

Feet pounded on the outside stairway, and the door flew open. Annabel rushed in, followed by Georgia and a couple of other people he didn't know but vaguely recognized from the birthday party. The Bodines were arriving in force. He backed away, giving them access to Miz Callie, divorcing himself from the family group.

He should leave. Amanda had her people here now, and she didn't need him.

But he'd given Hugh his cell number, so he couldn't very well go off without letting him know. More steps sounded on the stairs. A retreat was in order, if he didn't want to be inundated by Bodines.

He'd head into the kitchen and start some coffee. That was what people did while they waited for news, wasn't it? He'd make coffee and hope Hugh called soon.

He'd found the coffee and filters and started a pot when his cell phone rang. He jerked it out of his pocket. "Lockhart."

"Hugh Bodine here." It was a growl. "There's not much new, but I told my father I'd check in. How's Miz Callie doing?"

"Praying," he said. "She's handling it. Some other family came in."

Hugh grunted. "I can hear them in the background. That'll help, I guess. Just try to keep them focused on the positive. Adam's out there. He's not gonna come home without his cousin."

"I'll try." He hesitated, knowing he was involving himself still further, but feeling unable to stop. "Just between us, what are the chances?"

"Wish I knew. Win took a second life vest with him when he jumped. If he didn't lose it on the way down and managed to get it onto the victim, they can hang on for a time, warm as the water is."

"What if he lost it?"

"If he lost it, Win will give his vest to the victim." Hugh's flat tone suppressed a world of emotion.

"I see." He did. If Win was out there without a vest, trying to help two victims, with night falling…

"I've got to go," Hugh said quickly. "Hang in there. I'll get back to you when I can."

The call ended, and he hadn't told Hugh he was leaving.

Amanda came in, lifting her eyebrows when she saw the phone in his hand. "Was that Hugh?"

"Nothing new," he said quickly. "He just wanted to touch base."

If she thought he was hiding something, she didn't betray that. "Coffee. Good, thank you. I'll take some to Miz Callie." She stopped, hand on the cabinet door, and looked at him with such sweetness that it jolted him right in the heart. "Thank you for staying. It means a lot."

"No problem," he said, realizing the question had been decided for him. He was staying.

* * *

The beach house was beginning to crowd with people, reminding Amanda of a pot coming to a boil. Every Bodine was here except for Uncle Harrison and Aunt Miranda, Win's parents, who'd gone to the base along with anyone who had the credentials to get on base.

She was beginning to feel useless. To say nothing of the stress that bubbled along her nerves, threatening to explode.

Her gaze met Ross's. As if they'd communicated without words, he started making his way toward her.

Her heart gave an odd little twist. In spite of the unanswered questions that lay between them, he'd been a rock in this crisis, and she wasn't ashamed of clinging to him.

He stopped beside her, his dark brows lifting in a question.

"I can't stay here any longer. I've got to go down to the base."

"Can you get in?"

"Press credentials will do it. They might send me packing if I went alone, but they're not going to turn away the managing editor of the *Charleston Bugle*."

He gave a short nod. "Let's go."

It took minutes to explain to Miz Callie, and then she and Ross slipped away. Without seeming to think about it, he got into driver's seat.

Ordinarily that might raise her hackles, but not now. Today she needed to keep her thoughts, and her prayers, focused on Win.

Father, be with them. I know so many people are praying for them now. Please hear our prayers.

She glanced at Ross. She hadn't missed how uncomfortable he'd seemed at praying with them, and it had touched her heart when he'd taken her grandmother's hand with such tenderness.

"Thank you. I don't know how—"

He cut her off with a shake of his head. "Forget it."

The words were rough to the point of rudeness, but she sensed that they covered pain instead.

As if to fill the silence, Ross snapped the radio on, just in time for a local news bulletin about the rescue. She listened to it, fingers digging into her knees. Nothing that they didn't already know.

"They'll be trying to identify the missing rescue swimmer," Ross said.

"Yes." She swallowed, hating the thought of newspeople descending on her family while they waited. "Sometimes I don't like our profession much."

"Right."

They didn't speak again, and in a few minutes they'd reached the base. The procedure moved smoothly until they entered the building that housed the command center, where the press was being gently but firmly shepherded into a briefing room by Petty Officer Kelly Ryan.

Breathing a silent prayer of thanksgiving, Amanda caught her friend's eye and jerked her head toward the stairwell. Kelly gave the most minuscule of shrugs and nodded her head.

Grasping Ross's wrist, Amanda let the rest of the mob flow past them and led him quickly up the stairs. They reached the upper levels without incident.

"You'd make a good spy," Ross said.

"It helps to know the territory, but it's going to get harder now. If my father sees us…" She didn't need to finish that. Ross knew as well as she did what his reaction would be.

They'd just started down the hallway when an office door opened right in front of them. With no time to do anything else, Amanda met Thomas Morgan's startled gaze.

"Ms. Bodine." The young ensign who was her father's assistant glanced from her to Ross. "What are you doing here? The press is supposed be—"

She silenced him with an urgent hand on his arm. "That's my cousin out there. I can't just sit home waiting for news. You can help us, can't you, Tommy?"

His reluctance was palpable, reminding her that Daddy had said how intent his assistant was on promotion. Tommy wouldn't want to get into trouble.

"If we're caught, we won't say a word about you. Just get us someplace where we can know what's going on. Please."

He hesitated a moment longer, but then he shrugged. "Go up the next flight of steps and in the second door on the right. That's the best you'll be able to do without your father spotting you."

"Thanks." She squeezed his arm. "And we never saw you, right?"

"Right." Looking relieved, he backtracked into the office he'd come out of.

Following his directions, they reached the indicated door in moments. Amanda paused for a moment, refreshing her memory of the layout. If anyone she knew was on duty in the communications room, they'd probably be all right. Whispering a silent prayer, she opened the door and slipped inside.

The woman at the nearest station turned at their entrance. Thanking heaven for a familiar face, even if she couldn't come up with a name at the moment, Amanda gave her a pleading look.

With a hint of a smile, the woman turned back to her instruments as if she didn't see them.

"We're okay," she murmured to Ross.

He nodded, taking in the room with a thoughtful glance. "I was right. You can't go anywhere in Charleston without finding someone you know."

"It's really a small town, despite appearances." She watched the intent faces, longing for a sign. They were as tense as she was, focused on their jobs with lives in the balance. All the more so, because one of those lives was one of their own.

She fought to untangle the radio chatter she picked up, knowing that it must sound like so much gibberish to Ross.

"Reports are coming in from ships engaged in the search," she murmured quietly. "Negative, so far."

He clasped her hand warmly in his. "They'll find him."

She nodded, but dread began to pool in the pit of her stomach. The need for action had driven her this far, but what could she really accomplish here? Win was out there, somewhere. There was a lot of ocean to cover, and in a few hours it would be dark.

A hand went up, halfway down the row of technicians, beckoning to them. Amanda moved almost without awareness, grasping the back of his chair to steady herself. There was a chatter of static, and then a voice came through, identifying sender and location.

"That's Adam's patrol boat." She reached for Ross's hand, found it and gripped it hard.

The anonymous voice suddenly came through clearly. The room around them fell silent as others strained to hear.

"…have the wreckage in sight."

Please, Lord, please…

"Sighting two victims. Preparing to attempt the transfer."

Two. Where was the third? Win… Her heart seemed to stop. She felt Ross's arm go around her, supporting her.

Static. An endless wait. Static again. Then…

"Two victims, one rescue swimmer on board. All alive."

The room erupted in cheers. Amanda couldn't cheer. She could only sag against Ross, grateful for the strength of his arms around her.

Thank You, Lord. Thank You.

Chapter Fifteen

"This surely was one good news day." Cyrus looked down at the *Bugle,* spread across his massive oak desk and rubbed his palms together. The front page of the *Bugle* covered the rescue, lauding Win Bodine as a hero.

Which he was, Ross agreed. "We don't have a heroic story with a happy ending that often."

As Hugh had said he would, Win had given his life jacket to one of the victims and then managed to keep both of them safe and together until help arrived. You didn't get much more heroic than that.

"Those Bodines have more lives than a cat," Cyrus said. "Good thing, considering the jobs they go into."

"It's hard on the people who are waiting to hear if they're dead or alive." Ross would never forget the time he'd spent with Amanda and her grandmother yesterday. Never.

Amanda had leaned on him in a time of crisis. That was a sign of trust he hadn't expected, given how things had been between them recently.

That trust would be gone soon. He faced that bleakly. In a few days the story would break. Then she'd need all that strength she'd shown yesterday to get through the scandal.

She'd go through it with her head high. He had no doubt about that. But it would cut her to the bone, and she'd never be quite the same.

He'd like to say he'd give anything to protect her from that, but he couldn't. It wasn't true. He wouldn't give up his career.

He tried to assure himself that it wouldn't make a difference if he did. Cyrus would run the story anyway. Somehow that didn't make him feel any better.

"Too bad." Cyrus closed the paper and put it aside with an air of finality. "They're going to go from rejoicing today to grief tomorrow."

"Tomorrow?" That shook him. "You're surely not thinking to break the story that soon."

"There's no point in waiting that I can see." Cyrus's tone expressed sorrow laced with determination. "Besides, we've had the public's attention for the past few days. We can't afford to lose it at this point, you know that as well as I do."

Ross had rushed into print once before, eager to get the story out, and lived to regret that. At least this time he wasn't depending on anyone else's information, but even so, he wanted it ironclad before it went out with his byline. "Let's take it slower. We can't afford to make accusations without proof."

"We have the records of Winchell's contracts, one after another awarded to him by Bodine's office. We have the photos of the two of them meeting yesterday." Cyrus ticked off the facts.

He was being swept along too fast. "It's not enough. There's no law against the two of them meeting at the festival, despite appearances."

Cyrus's shaggy eyebrows lifted. "What about the packet?"

Ross felt as if he'd missed a step in the dark. "Packet?"

"Didn't you look at the pictures you took?" Apparently taking the answer for granted, Cyrus grabbed a folder from his desk, shaking the contents out onto the surface. "Look. If that's not incriminating, I don't know what is."

Ross took the photo Cyrus held out and saw

the thing he'd completely missed in his efforts to get as many shots as he could. Winchell, holding out a bulky envelope to Brett Bodine.

Wordlessly, Cyrus passed him another. In this shot, Bodine was stuffing the envelope into his jacket pocket. Maybe that explained why the man had been wearing a jacket on such a hot day.

"I never saw them." He shook his head. "Just snapped as many as I could get without being seen. With everything that happened afterward, I…"

He'd been too busy worrying about Amanda. Trying to help her in any way he could. And all the time, the proof about her father was in the camera he carried.

Here was the big story he'd been looking for since he came to the *Bugle*. A step back toward the life he wanted.

So why wasn't he happier?

Amanda entered the newsroom later than her usual time, but with a light step. The family had been up until all hours, rejoicing over Win's safe return.

Of course Win had wanted to downplay it, so they'd tried to go along, but tears had never been far from the surface.

"Amanda!" C.J. was the first to spot her, and

she came at a half run to envelop her in a hug. "Nobody thought you'd come in today."

"I didn't think that." Jim elbowed C.J. over to get in on the hug, pressing his cheek against Amanda's. "I knew all along that this gal was a pro. Glad everything turned out okay, sugar."

Those treacherous tears threatened to spill over again. "We are, too. Thanks, Jim."

The rest of the newsroom staff had gathered around her by then, wanting to share in the happiness, and her heart swelled. It really did feel as if all of Charleston had been praying with them and now shared their happiness. That had been the message on the flowers Miz Callie received that morning from Cyrus, coming so early that he must have had to wake up the florist.

Flowers for joy, not for condolence. A shudder went through her at the thought of how easily it could have gone the other way.

She pulled back, squeezing C.J.'s hand. "Thanks, everyone, so much. I just can't tell you how much it helped to know folks were praying with us." She wiped away a tear that had escaped. "I've got to thank Cyrus, too, and then I'd best get back to work."

She escaped down the hall that led to Cyrus's office, blotting her eyes with a tissue. Maybe in a day or two she'd have gotten over this tendency to cry at the least little thing. Though even time probably wouldn't erase the memory of those hours when they hadn't known whether Win was alive or dead.

She couldn't think of that without thinking of Ross. He'd stayed with her through it all. At the time she hadn't even questioned turning to him in the crisis. It had seemed the most natural thing in the world. For all his sharp edges and occasional cynicism, he'd been a rock when she needed him.

Oh, she'd have gotten through it without him. She had her family and her faith to see her through. Her heart chilled. Ross didn't seem to have either of those. Small wonder that he'd turned cynic.

Maybe she could make a difference. Things had been rocky between them, but maybe, given time and patience, there could be a future for them. After yesterday's seemingly miraculous rescue, she could believe in another happy ending, couldn't she?

Cyrus's door stood ajar, and she paused, hearing voices. He had someone with him. She'd have to come back later.

Then she realized that the second voice

belonged to Ross, and her heart gave a silly little leap. Smiling, she reached toward the door.

"…the Bodine story." Ross's voice was a low rumble. They must be talking about the coverage of Win's rescue.

"The photo of Brett Bodine has to go above the fold on page one." Cyrus's voice rang out clearly. "Showing him accepting the bribe tells the whole story in a single picture."

Her breath caught in her throat, feeling as if it would strangle her. Brett…bribe…what on earth were they talking about? Those two words didn't belong in the same sentence.

"…seems pretty clear," Ross was saying.

Ross…plotting against Daddy. Her heart seemed caught in a vise that tightened cruelly as she tried to comprehend what she was hearing.

Her fingers closed on the edge of the door. She'd confront them, tell them—

Wait. Stop and think. She took a steadying breath, then another. Pulled her hand away from the door.

That was always her default reaction, wasn't it? Rush in without thinking.

Not this time. Not if Daddy was in trouble and Ross was his betrayer. The vise on her heart gave another, stronger twist.

She had to find out what they were planning so she'd know what she was fighting. There had to be a logical explanation for this. Would Jim know?

She rejected that. Jim was many things, but not much of an actor. He couldn't have greeted her the way he had if he'd been in on a story that would discredit her father.

No, this had Ross's fingerprints all over it. Ross had been lying the whole time he'd been supporting her. Comforting her. Kissing her.

Her cheeks flamed. She had to find out the truth. She backed silently away from the door and headed for Ross's office.

There'd be no euphoria at the breaking of this story, Ross knew. Just a dogged determination to do his job, coupled with a bone-deep despair over what that was going to do to Amanda.

God, if You're there, if You still listen to me, help her.

Once this broke, she wouldn't appreciate the thought that he prayed for her. The dagger in his heart dug a little deeper.

Could he warn her? Totally unprofessional, but how could he let her be blindsided?

He swung his office door open and froze in his tracks. Amanda wouldn't be blindsided. She stood at his desk, reading the file of notes on the investigation.

She looked at him, face white, eyes blazing, and shook a sheet of paper at him. "How can you possibly believe this? You've met my father. He wouldn't do anything like this."

He closed the door behind him. No one else needed to know what they'd say to each other.

"I wouldn't have thought you'd go through my desk, either. Looks like we're both wrong." But the indignation he tried to drum up rang hollow.

Twin flags of scarlet burned in her cheeks. "I was coming to Cyrus's office to talk to him. To thank him for the flowers he sent to my grandmother. And guess what I heard? You and Cyrus planning a front-page story framing my father."

"We're not framing anyone." He took a step closer, trying to keep his voice low. Trying to keep some control over the situation. "We're not printing anything but the truth. If you wanted the truth, you should have asked us, not come searching in my desk."

"I had to know what I was fighting." She slapped the paper down on the stack.

"There's no fighting about it. The decision has already been made. The story runs tomorrow." He reached toward her, knowing she didn't want him anywhere near her, but unable to stop the gesture. "At least you're forewarned now."

"Forewarned?" Her voice rose. She was teetering on the edge. Hardly surprising after everything that had happened the previous day. "You're going to print lies about my father. Don't you know that will destroy his career? And the family…" She stopped, her voice breaking.

"I'm sorry for all the people who are going to be hurt." She probably didn't believe that. "But you have to realize that your father's the one who brought this down on you. Not the newspaper."

"He's innocent. He would never—"

"Look." He pulled the condemning photograph from the folder he held. "Just look at it and accept the truth. That's your father taking money from a contractor who's gotten way more than his fair share of business from the base, thanks to your father's influence."

The picture shook her. He could see that in the way her eyes darkened and her lips pressed together as she tried to assimilate the pain.

Her reaction shook him, too. The need to comfort her nearly overwhelmed him. Yesterday she'd leaned on him, and he'd been there for her. Today—

Today he could do nothing.

She shook her head, thrusting the picture away from her. "There's an explanation. There has to be. Just talk to him."

"I can't."

"Why not? You at least interviewed that slumlord before you ran the story."

"This is Cyrus's decision, not mine. I'm an employee of this paper, just as you are."

"Not anymore." She straightened, bracing herself with her fingertips on his desk for a moment, and then walking around it toward the door, avoiding him as she might a skunk in the road.

"Amanda—" But what could he say? Naturally she wouldn't keep working here after this.

"It's funny." She paused, hand on the doorknob. "I spent all this time trying to show you that you were wrong about me." She turned to face him. "But maybe you were right all along. I really am that sweet Southern girl you thought I was. And my family is more important to me than anything else."

She yanked the door open and walked out of his office and out of his life.

Chapter Sixteen

She'd been looking for her father for hours without success. Amanda's stomach churned as she picked up her cell phone to try once more. Why wasn't he picking up? If she didn't get to him in time to stop that story from going to press…

The call went immediately to messages. Gritting her teeth, she ended the call. Little point in adding yet another "where are you?" to the ones she'd already recorded.

She crossed her tiny living room in five steps and stared out the front window, catching a group of tourists with cameras pointed in her direction.

Letting the curtain fall between them, she took a deep breath. A few tourists was nothing compared to the crowd that would descend on

Mamma and Daddy's house if that story ran. She couldn't let that happen.

She picked up the phone again. Time to bring in the big guns. She hadn't wanted to call Mamma, fearing her mother would read the anxiety in her tone, but she couldn't waste any more time, not when her mental clock ticked away the hours until the paper went to press.

"Mamma? Hi, it's Manda."

"Sugar, what's goin' on with you? How about comin' over for supper tomorrow? I'm making Brunswick stew."

"That sounds great, Mamma. Maybe I will." Or maybe they'd all be too busy dealing with fallout to eat. "Right now I need to get hold of Daddy. He's not picking up his cell phone. Do you know where he is?"

"Goodness, I…I don't know. He had to go out this evening, but I don't believe he said…"

"Mamma, this is important." She couldn't keep up the facade that was just a casual call, not when the need for action pounded in her brain and tightened every muscle. "Where is he?"

"Sugar, you make it sound like life and death." A thread of uneasiness laced her mother's voice.

She took a breath and sent up a wordless prayer that she wasn't making things worse. "It's important. You and Daddy don't keep secrets from each other, no matter what he says. Whatever he's involved in, the newspaper is about to blow it wide-open. I've got to get to him."

Silence for a long moment. "He's at Battery Park, meeting with…someone."

She suppressed the urge to press for more answers. Time enough for that once she'd found Daddy. "Thanks, Mamma." She hung up and darted for the door.

A few minutes later she was pulling into a parking space bordering the park. She could have walked, but if she missed Daddy here, she'd waste time running back for her car. She stepped up the high curb and stood on the sidewalk, surveying the park.

Battery Park, covering the end of the peninsula that was Charleston, was a popular tourist destination, but by now most of them had probably headed for dinner or back to their hotels to put their feet up. Stilling her nervous impulse to rush through the park, she stood where she was, scanning the area methodically.

No sign of him, and her heart sank. Time was running out. If she—

There he was, leaning against the wall, looking out over the water toward Fort Sumter. Another man stood next to him. Not, she realized with relief, the contractor who'd been in the photo Ross showed her.

She hurried across the grass toward them, her heartbeat quickening as she approached. How did she say this? How could she tell her father that the world was about to hear he was a liar and a thief?

The other man saw her first, and she saw the quick flare of recognition in his eyes before he turned away to point out in the general direction of Sullivan's Island.

How did he know who she was? She'd never seen him before. Casually dressed, middle-aged. Military, she thought automatically. When you were around it all the time, you knew.

"Daddy."

He turned around. "Amanda. What are you doing here?"

"Looking for you. We have to talk."

The other man spoke up. "Thanks for the sight-seeing tips. I'll be sure to check out the places you mentioned."

"What? Oh, yes." Daddy was rattled. "Glad I could be of help."

Too late, she thought. She'd seen that betraying look of recognition. Whatever was going on, this was no casual meeting. This man was in on it.

"It's no good," she said. "I know."

"Honey, now's not a good time. How about I stop by your place in a little bit, okay?"

She shook her head. There was nothing to do but come out with it.

"The *Bugle* is after you," she said flatly. "They're running a story in tomorrow's paper. They've got a picture of you at the festival taking money from some contractor." She got it all out on a rush of words and came to a stop, feeling as if she'd been running.

Her breath caught in her throat. Daddy looked dismayed. Not guilty, thank the good Lord. Just unhappy with the news she'd brought.

She grasped his hand, feeling the strength of it close around hers as it had when she was a little girl. She blinked back tears.

"I know you didn't do anything wrong. You couldn't have. But unless you do something to stop it, all Charleston is going to read about that in tomorrow's paper."

Still holding her hand, her father looked at the other man. "What do you think?"

For a moment the man's face tightened in denial. Then he shrugged. "I guess we'd better go down to the newspaper and resolve this."

* * *

"That's it, then." Ross stared across the width of the office at Cyrus, the weight of the decision pressing on him. "I'll…"

The rap on the door gave him a welcome respite. "Come in," he called, despite Cyrus's frown.

Brett Bodine stalked in, followed by another man—lean, graying, with a closed face that gave nothing away. Bodine, with his flushed face and clenched jaw, was easier to read. He'd like to take Ross's head off.

Ross thrust his chair backward as he rose. If Bodine thought he could intimidate the press—

The thought broke off when he saw who else was there. Amanda. A quick glance was all he could allow himself, but even that was like a blow in the gut.

Cyrus took a step forward, the light of battle in his eyes. "If you're here to talk us out of the story, you've come to the wrong place."

Bodine's hands curled into fists, but before he could speak, the other man interrupted, pulling an ID from his pocket. "This isn't precisely what you think, gentlemen."

He held it out to Cyrus. Whatever it was, it stopped him cold. He looked, grunted, and passed it to Ross with an air of handing the situation over to him.

"Agent Baker." He let the realization sink in. "What's the federal government want from the *Bugle?*"

Baker permitted himself the briefest of smiles. "Ordinarily, nothing. But Ms. Bodine told us about the story you plan to break."

He couldn't prevent his gaze from slipping to Amanda. She hadn't known about the federal agent, he could see that.

He forced his focus back to the agent, preparing to negotiate. This was familiar territory, after all. He'd often played the game of getting as much information as possible from tight-lipped officials.

"And what exactly is your interest in our story?"

"We'd prefer that you refrain from printing it."

Ross sensed Cyrus's feathers ruffling at that, but the older man kept silent. With a little luck, he'd let Ross handle this.

"I'm afraid we can't accommodate you." Ross's mind worked furiously, trying to sort out the possibilities. Bodine might be cooperating with the feds, ready to give up his fellow conspirators. In that case, they could be playing for time.

"I'm not trying to pressure you, Mr. Lockhart.

Only to prevent the *Bugle* and you from making an embarrassing mistake."

Ross stiffened at the expression, but kept a slight smile pinned to his face. It was all part of the elaborate dance, with Baker determined to give away as little as possible while Ross was equally set on getting the whole story.

"It's good of you to be concerned for the *Bugle,* but you'll have to convince us with facts."

"Tell him and be done with it," Bodine snarled. "He's not going to cooperate for less."

"Daddy…" Amanda began, and then stopped, hands moving in a small gesture of helplessness.

The gesture seemed to clutch his heart. For a moment he could barely breathe for the desperate need to protect her.

Agent Baker shrugged. "You realize that this is off-the-record." He looked from Cyrus to Ross. Seeming satisfied with their nods, he went on. "Several months ago, we received a report of possible irregularities in the awarding of contracts at the Coast Guard base here. The report came from Brett Bodine."

A small gasp escaped Amanda.

"We investigated." Baker went on as if he

hadn't heard. "With his assistance, we were able to identify the officer involved."

The facts Ross thought he knew flew into the air, rearranged themselves and came down in a new pattern. "But the meeting with Winchell. The packet of money."

"Not money," Baker said. "We've managed to persuade Mr. Winchell to cooperate with us. He handed over a list of the deals made by the officer."

Bodine's expression tightened, if that was possible, and Ross understood. The man was in pain at the idea that someone under his command had abused his position.

"We need you to kill the story until we've completed our investigation," Baker said. "I can assure you, it's in your country's best interest."

"Who is the guilty party?" Ross planted both hands on the desk. Baker had to give them more than that.

"I can't tell you that."

"You can give us an exclusive," Ross countered. "If we don't jump the gun on you, that's the least you can do."

Baker's noncommittal mask was probably hiding some furious calculating. How far could he go?

"Forty-eight hours," he said at last. "You don't mention anything in the press for forty-eight hours, and we'll give you a couple hours' head start on the story. That's the best I can do."

"It's a deal," Cyrus said, clearly unable to contain himself any longer.

"Good." Baker shook hands briskly, first with Cyrus, then with him. "We'll be in touch."

Bodine took the hand Cyrus extended. For Ross, he had nothing but a furious glare. And Amanda…tears had spilled over, trickling down her cheeks.

Bodine and Baker turned to the door, Cyrus behind them, probably trying to get another fragment or two about the story.

He didn't bother to listen. All he could see, all he could think of, was Amanda. He reached out, not quite daring to touch her.

"Amanda, please. Stay. Just for a moment."

Her father spun at the words. "My daughter has nothing to say to you."

Amanda wiped away tears with the palm of her hand. "It's all right, Daddy. I'll be along in a few minutes."

She closed the door behind them and turned to face him.

* * *

She didn't want to stay. Amanda pressed her palms against the solid wood of the door behind her. Talking to Ross was only going to make the pain in her heart worse. But she wouldn't be a coward about it.

Ross's face was a taut mask, revealing nothing of the feelings behind it. If any. Did he feel anything but ambition? Want anything but success?

A cold shudder went through her. "There's no point to this." She turned away, groping for the doorknob.

"Wait. Please. You need to see something."

She didn't move.

"Please." His voice softened to a husky rumble. "Just look at this, and I won't ask you for anything more."

She turned back slowly to face him, and he swung his computer screen toward her.

"Look. This is the front page of tomorrow's edition, made up before we heard the agent's story."

She had to brace herself before she could look at it. Had to prepare herself to see the photo of Daddy. Above the fold, Cyrus had said.

She stared. Blinked. And took a step toward him, shaking her head to clear it.

"What? Where is it?" The lead story was a

follow-up to the rescue. She leaned closer, scanning the page. Nothing. There was no mention of anything else to do with the Coast Guard Base.

She touched the screen, reading it through to be sure she wasn't making any mistake. Then she looked up at Ross's face.

"I don't understand. You were going to run the story in tomorrow's edition. Why did you give it up before you'd even heard the explanation? Did Cyrus change his mind?"

"Not Cyrus. I changed my mind. Cyrus...well, he went along with me in the end."

Meaning Cyrus hadn't wanted to. She tried to still the spinning of her mind. Tried to hold out against the hope that began to blossom inside her.

"You convinced him not to run the story. Why?"

He turned away slightly, as if he didn't want her to see his face. His fingers pressed against the desktop until they were white.

"You." He stopped, cleared his throat. "When I saw how much you were hurt, it forced me to take a good look at myself." He darted a glance toward her. "I didn't like what I saw. The man my grandmother had hoped I'd be—he's pretty well buried by now, isn't he?"

He didn't seem to expect an answer to that, which was fortunate, because she didn't have one.

"I've been blaming everyone else for what happened to me back in D.C., but the truth is that a major part of the blame falls squarely on me."

That she could respond to. "Your friend betrayed you. That wasn't your fault."

"I'm the one who fell for it. I'm the one who rushed into print. I was too proud, too sure of myself." The muscles in his neck moved convulsively. "I never stopped to ask myself whether I might be wrong."

The chill that had gripped her heart began to fall away. Ross was taking down his protective barriers, piece by piece. He was letting her see who he really was.

"My grandmother expected me to become an honorable man who relied on God for guidance. Instead, I became a cynic who relied on nothing but his own ambition. That's not who I want to be."

He was facing her now, close enough that she could see the pain that darkened his eyes and twisted his lips.

"No," she said softly. "It isn't who you are, not really." She tapped the computer screen. "You put your job on the line with Cyrus to delay the story, even before you knew the truth."

"Cyrus thought I was crazy." He shook his head. "Crazy was what I was before, when I let myself be eaten up by anger and ambition. Maybe being humbled by losing everything I thought was important was the only road back to finding out who I really am."

Tears spilled over again, but they were good tears. "I'm sorry you went through that. But if you hadn't, I'd never have met you."

"Maybe you'd be better off if you hadn't."

"Don't say that." She hesitated, wanting to put into words the effect he'd had on her. "Being challenged by you made me realize what's really important to me."

He reached out slowly, letting his fingers brush her cheek. Warmth flooded through her, erasing the last bit of tension.

"I already know. Your family. Your faith. Any chance there's room for me on that list?"

She couldn't breathe for the happiness that filled her, bubbling up until she felt she might lift off the floor. "There's plenty of room for you."

"I love you, Amanda Bodine."

She caught his hand, pressed it against her lips and said the words. "I love you, Ross."

"Enough to marry me?" There was the faintest trace of uncertainty in the words.

"Definitely," she said.

He drew her against him, his lips claiming hers in a kiss that promised a love that would last a lifetime. Her arms went around him, holding him close, knowing this was meant to be. God had planned them for each other from the beginning. They'd just both been too stubborn to see it.

Ross pressed his cheek against hers. "My grandmother would be delighted."

Joy bubbled up in her again. "Miz Callie will be, too."

He held her back a little so that she could see the love burning steadily in his eyes. "I'm afraid your father is not going to be exactly pleased."

"He'll come around when he sees how happy you make me," she said. "He'll see that God meant us for each other. Forever."

Epilogue

Miz Callie had insisted on a family dinner to celebrate Amanda's unexpected engagement. Amanda wasn't so sure that was a good idea. Maybe it would have been better to wait until everyone had gotten used to it—in this case, everyone being her father.

Still, so far they all seemed to be behaving themselves. Against Miz Callie's will, everyone had brought something, with the result that there was enough food spread out on the long table at the beach house to feed half the island.

Since they'd long since outgrown the number of available tables, folks had spread out all over the place, and the volume of Bodine chatter was faintly overwhelming, even to someone who was as used to it as she was.

She glanced at Ross, sitting next to her on the living-room floor. He smiled, seeming unaffected by the clamor, and leaned over to kiss her cheek lightly.

"Everything okay?" he asked.

"Very much okay." She moved a little closer. "You're officially accepted, I do believe."

"More or less," he said, but it didn't seem to bother him that Daddy wasn't quite reconciled.

"Of course you're accepted." Miz Callie, sitting behind them in her favorite rocker, touched Ross lightly on the head. "Brett is even being pleasant."

"Maybe he's just relieved that this investigation is wrapped up and moved off the front page," Ross suggested.

"Well, now, I wouldn't be surprised." Miz Callie's face clouded a little. "He took it hard, knowing that an officer under his command betrayed the service that way."

They'd all been shocked to learn that her father's aide, Thomas Morgan, had been using his position to take money under the table from contractors in exchange for doctoring the bids.

"Nobody wants to hear that a fellow officer is crooked." Adam, arms wrapped around his knees, leaned forward to join the conversation. "That's someone you might have to trust your life to one day, besides the fact that it gives all the honest men and women in the service a black eye."

"I think most folks know enough not to blame anyone else for what one person did." Miz Callie rested her hand on Amanda's shoulder. "As for us, I'd say we have a lot to celebrate."

She'd raised her voice a little on the words, and the room seemed to fall silent as she spoke. Miz Callie's descendants turned their faces toward her.

"We celebrate our Win's safety after a dangerous mission."

Win smiled, looking a little embarrassed as sounds of thanksgiving echoed through the room.

"We celebrate the fact that truth has come out in a difficult situation." She looked at Amanda's father, her eyes bright with unshed tears. "Your daddy would be proud of you, Brett. You did your duty."

More than one person blinked back tears, Amanda knew. They realized, none better, just how hard that had been for her father.

"And we celebrate the truth coming out about another family member who did his duty." Now a tear did trickle down Miz Callie's cheek, but her hand on Amanda's shoulder was strong. "We know now that Ned Bodine served his country in the navy during the war, and he's going to be honored as he should be for that service. Adam has learned that Ned didn't die in the war."

A murmur of surprise went through the room at that. Most of them had just assumed that Ned hadn't come back.

"We'll find out what became of him afterward, Miz Callie." Ross took her hand. "I promise."

Miz Callie touched Amanda and Ross, her touch seeming to link them to all the generations that had gone before. "And we share the happiness of Amanda and Ross. May their love grow and flourish all their days."

Amanda let her gaze move from one face to another around the room—her kin, the people she knew best in the world, linked by faith and by love. She had them, and now she had Ross. Her heart was filled to overflowing with thankfulness.

* * * * *

Don't miss the next Bodine family romance,
from beloved author Marta Perry
On sale July 2010,
from Steeple Hill Love Inspired.

Dear Reader,

Thank you for choosing to pick up the second book in my new Love Inspired series about the Bodine family of South Carolina. Amanda Bodine takes center stage in this story as she struggles to find her place in the world, defend her family and commit to true love.

Amanda and her hero, Ross, are both searching for the secret to who they really are and what God wants for them. I'm sure many of us have walked that road, wondering whether we're really on the path God intends. I hope you'll identify with Amanda's struggles.

I hope you'll let me know how you felt about this story. I'd love to send you a signed bookmark or my brochure of Pennsylvania Dutch recipes. You can write to me at Steeple Hill Books, 223 Broadway, Suite 1001, New York, NY 10279, e-mail me at marta@martaperry.com, or visit me on the Web at www.martaperry.com.

Blessings,

Marta Perry

QUESTIONS FOR DISCUSSION

1. Can you understand why Amanda was troubled by the doubts she felt about her life choices when she turned thirty? Have you struggled with any of the landmark birthdays? If so, how did you resolve those feelings?

2. Amanda's personality leads her to become a sister to anyone in trouble. Is that always a good reaction? Can you think of a time in which that might backfire on a person?

3. Amanda, like Georgia in the first book of this series, finds that everyone in her family has an opinion as to what she should do. Had this ever happened to you? How do you sort out God's calling from the demands of others?

4. Ross is so caught up in his anger over what happened to him in the past that he can't see his present clearly. How do you deal with it when you can't forget a hurt?

5. Ross drifted away from his early faith in God after his grandmother's death. Have you

ever experienced that? If so, how did you come back to God?

6. The scripture verse for this story reminds us to put God first in all that we do. How do you feel about doing that? Is it difficult to do that in the press of your daily life and experiences?

7. Amanda finds it difficult to confront Ross initially, but she finds the courage to do it when other people's happiness is at stake. Has that ever happened to you, causing you to feel that you had to confront someone over their behavior? How can you do that in a Christ-like manner?

8. Why do you think C.J is so antagonistic to Amanda at first? Should Amanda have done anything differently with her?

9. Amanda's grandmother longs to find the truth about the past. Do you think it's always a good idea to do that?

10. Did you sympathize with Ross's need to get back the life he's lost? How might he have handled the situation better?

11. In the end, Ross realizes that he was to blame in part for the situation that caused him to lose his job. Why is it so difficult for him to face that?

12. Ross also comes to realize that if he hadn't gone through the bad times, he'd never have turned back to God. Do you think God can use the difficulties we encounter to help us to turn to Him? Has that ever happened to you?

13. Which character in the story did you feel was living the most Christ-like life? Why?

14. How do you feel about Win's decisions during the rescue effort? Does he do the right thing?

15. In the end, Amanda feels that she and Ross have discovered their "true colors," the people they are at a soul-deep level. Do you think that some people never really understand themselves? Do you think that people change who they really are at bottom?

*Read on for a sneak preview of
KATIE'S REDEMPTION
by Patricia Davids,
the first book in the heartwarming new
BRIDES OF AMISH COUNTRY series
available in March 2010
from Steeple Hill Love Inspired.*

*When a pregnant formerly Amish woman
returns to her brother's house, seeking
forgiveness and a place to give birth
to her child, what she finds there
isn't what she expected.*

*P*lease, God, don't let them send me away.

To give her child a home Katie Lantz would
endure the angry tirade she expected from her
brother. Through it all Malachi wouldn't be able
to hide the gloating in his voice.

An unexpected tightening across her stomach
made Katie suck in a quick breath. She'd been
up since dawn, riding for hours on the jolting bus.

Her stomach tightened again. The pain
deepened. Something wasn't right. This was
more than fatigue. It was labor.

Breathing hard, she peered through the blowing snow. It wasn't much farther to her brother's farm. Closing her eyes, she gathered her strength.

One foot in front of the other. The only way to finish a journey is to start it.

She sagged with relief when her hand closed over the railing. She was home.

Home. The word echoed inside her mind, bringing with it unhappy memories that pushed aside her relief. Raising her fist, she knocked at the front door. Then she bowed her head and closed her eyes, grasping the collar of her coat to keep the chill at bay.

When the door finally opened, she looked up to meet her brother's gaze.

Katie sucked in a breath and then took a half step back. A tall, broad-shouldered Amish man stood in front of her with a kerosene lamp in his hand and a faintly puzzled expression on his handsome face.

It wasn't Malachi.

To read more of Katie's story, pick up
KATIE'S REDEMPTION
by Patricia Davids,
available March 2010.

Love Inspired ®
SUSPENSE
RIVETING INSPIRATIONAL ROMANCE

Watch for our new series of
edge-of-your-seat suspense novels.
These contemporary tales
of intrigue and romance
feature Christian characters
facing challenges to their faith...
and their lives!

NOW AVAILABLE IN REGULAR
& LARGER-PRINT FORMATS

Steeple
Hill®

Visit:
www.SteepleHill.com